Circumambulate

CIRCUMAMBULATE
Copyright © Serpent Club Press, 2015

Serpent Club Press books may be purchased for educational, business, or sales
promotional use. For more information please contact Serpent Club Press at
theserpentclub@gmail.com

First Edition

Printed in the United States of America
Set in Williams Caslon
Designed by Emily Gasda

ISBN
9780990664345

LCCN
2015945223

Circumambulate

A novel by Daniel Bossert

Serpent Club Press

Other works from Serpent Club Press:

2013
Moon on Water
Matthew Gasda

2014
Autumn, Again; Spring, Anew
Michael Skelton and Stephen Morel

On Bicycling: An Introduction
Samuel Atticus Steffen

2015
Sonata for Piano and Violin
Matthew Gasda

New Writing: Volume 1
A Compilation

Circumambulate
Daniel Bossert

The Bacchae
Matthew Gasda

Contents

Thank you, from the bottom of my heart—for I could not have made it without you, without having loved you as much as I did, for M——, believe me, believe me, please, even if these are only words, and they can't tell you what I really feel, that I loved you, as much as I could...

Know Thyself

One of the great lessons of Socrates was the unnnecessity of having *fear* when one looked death full in the face. When his friends—or, as they would have called themselves, his followers—asked him why, in that moment, he was not *afraid* (as most every man would be), his response had to do with the immortality of the soul, and the mistake of fearing something which—in fact—could only bring about a greater good.

Yet it is not this explanation—the philosophical justification he gives—for his lack of fear towards death, which has made him (and this anecdote) so famous throughout all of Western civilization. It was the stance and the *feeling* of not fearing death—one so powerfully described by Plato—that has lasted (for so long) as something to be striven towards or *emulated*. The Epicureans said the same sort of thing, but their stance was so superficial, and used death in such a contrasting, metaphorical way—*enjoy life while it's here; don't fear death, because you won't be there to feel it*. Socrates' lack of fear towards death always seemed to me so much deeper, so much wiser and more *valuable* than that of his successors.

For me, I think part of the reason is what the image, the character, the *figure* of Socrates stands for—that notoriously ugly old man, who nonetheless attracted the most beautiful and coveted youths; the gadfly of Athens, who had no greater passion that in proving others *foolish* (the higher up in society, the better); the accused, who presented no real defense, and who never—no matter how *easy* it would have been—considered escaping; the individual who was prophesized as the wisest of all men, precisely because (as he knew) he recognized more than any other man how *little* he knew.

Socrates' whole life was a dedication to *doubt*, to the act of questioning and of never fully admitting something as a final, definitive end. Above all, this meant that Socrates always maintained the slightest hint of *separation* from all things. The perpetual distance within his own spheres of intimacy—with his wife, who he hated and probably avoided going home to; with his children, the fruit of his loins whom he seems to have cared little for; with all the youths who were obsessed with him, whom he gladly taught but never once would sleep with—shows us this, as do the various other things we know of him: he could drink endless quantities of alcohol—as much as was given to him—without becoming drunk; his ugliness, and the instantaneous way it would *repel* the gaze, in the same manner that beauty would have *attracted* it; the manner in which he handled his trial, as if it were nothing more than a *farce* for him to watch; the way he did not even *submit* to his death sentence, so much as continue to live—in Athens—as he had always done, unrepentant towards the changes in the situation which could only lead (inevitably) to his death. If this distance is what his *life* fundamentally consisted of, why should his *death* be any different?

For me, Socrates's *courage* towards death (for lack of fear—in such a moment—is perhaps as courageous as man can be) did not arise from the belief he had about the immortality of his soul, and the inconsequentiality—except for the better—of his death. Rather, my Socrates courageously stares death in the face because he remains—as always—slightly *detached* from everything, perpetually aware that what he sees and what he knows is (and always will be) severely limited to the tiny domain of the *human* and the *personal*. For all he knows, death could be anything—anything, at *all*—and he has no prior experience, nor is there any testimony of others, which could persuade the doubt he carries always inside himself to falter. Not even death could convince him to slip into beliefs or certainties—of expectation or hope, dread or *fear*—of this thing, this *thing* which (like every other thing he has ever encountered) remains for him a vague and ultimately impenetrable stronghold, which he has no ambitions to try to siege. Socrates abstains from all certainties, as he has always done—too aware of his *own* limits, and the limits of all *humans*—leaving knowledge and truth to the *gods*, who could know them (and handle them) in a way that no *mortal* ever could.

This is not to say that Socrates, himself—at times—did not fall prey to the temptations of betraying his *doubt*. Even with the influence of his *daemon* warning him of what not to do—holding him back from crossing that consummate distance from all things, which made him what he was, and which also made him *wise*—Socrates was still human. At times, he may have tried to describe his feelings, but language and his moods (carelessness, fatigue, melancholy) lead him into the traps into which all humans fall, seeming to speak of certain *realities* when all that we know are the hazy, nebulous interpretations we give of our feelings— the doubtful *stories* we weave around everything, in our lives. To put it simply: his *feeling* was true, but the justification of it (I often muse) was— possibly—*imperfect*.

I am no one, and I will not question Socrates' words, above all not these words given so freely from his deathbed. But I often imagine that Socrates— that master of both doubt and *self-awareness*— was nonetheless trapped by the peril into which everyone is born: being unable—without some sort of assistance—to see your own *face*. Perhaps

Socrates was no exception to the slight surprise that always overtakes us, when the face we *imagine* we have never matches—exactly—the one that we see before us in our reflection.

When Socrates, earlier in his life, spoke of the way that all knowledge is a sort of *remembrance*, he has recourse—once again—to the idea of the soul's immortality, in order to try to explain and justify his statement. But if Socrates (as I like to picture him) does not wholeheartedly admit these things— nor any things, whether they be ideas or people— into the *distance* he keeps around himself, then what we see is a Socrates who wishes to express his insights, but whose words instead convey something imperfectly reminiscent of what he actually *feels*. Socrates has once (or perhaps many times) experienced the feeling that—in gaining some new sort of *knowledge*—*memory* deeply infused all of it. As if he were reaching back towards something already *inside* him, already in his *past*— finding (once again) something he has *lost*, but had forgotten losing. The insight and the *feeling* were true—that all knowledge comes from memory— something which few other individuals throughout history have had the self-awareness to put into words. Yet, the interpretation that Socrates gave of it—and the *message* that appears to be passed down, when reading the dialogues—misleads one towards some sort of *belief,* and away from Socrates' consummate state of *doubt*. That doubt—unceasing and ineffable—which Socrates holds onto in his *life,* but not always in his *explanations*.

Which takes us back, once again, to that scene in the *Phaedo*, in which Socrates—infused by (and aware of) his lack of fear towards death—is asked to explain his feelings, and responds with the philosophical doctrine of the soul's *immortality*. I do not know if Socrates actually believed this idea—if he were (in his last moments) showing his true colors, or simply entertaining that deathbed conversion we so often hear spoken of. Yet, I don't think it would matter, either way. Putting my cards on the table—I don't believe in the *immortality* of the soul. (But I wouldn't *disbelieve* it, either...) And for me, Socrates—this character who, in his thorough dedication to doubt, always treats life as more a *dream* than a *reality*, something so circumscribed by *unknowing* that the least foolish we can be is to admit our own, perpetual *ignorance*—would feel the same. Death wouldn't scare him, because death (like all of life) remains forever beyond what he can *know*, in his earthly days. He is not afraid, because only in *dying* will he know what death is—perhaps not even then. Perhaps he will never reach any sort of certainty, never leave behind—even in *death*—that undercurrent of doubt which slips (unnoticed by everyone else) under all the things he encounters, day after day. This does not scare him, though— death shouldn't be feared or hoped for, avoided or sought out. For that would involve knowing what *death* is. And he doesn't know. He doesn't know *anything*. (*You are a ridiculous human being...*) Which is the only thing he *does* know...

06.11.11, 01.17.13

I've long said that dreams, for me, were like *correctives*. In the manner of Socrates's *daemon*, they only appear—or, at least, they only carry over into consciousness—in order to tell me what *not* to do.

When I remember my dreams (for I don't usually remember them), there are fundamentally two reactions that I have: either I—*dangerously*—never want to wake up from them; or I know, almost immediately—in that half-lucid state, before waking—that I need to find a *corrective*, both in the dream and in my life. The first are dreams that I fall in *love* with—flighty, airy nothings that captivate me—and I never want to return to reality without them. I do not care if they aren't *real*: they are more alive—more *perfect*—than anything I have ever felt before, and I never want to leave them behind. The other dreams are those that immediately strike me as needing *correction*, revealing something about myself that is painful or *unpleasant* to see. There was a time when all I dreamt about was traveling and airports. In the dreams, I was trying to leave a given place, but there were always things popping up that prevented me (or gave me the *excuse*) from actually getting on the plane and leaving. These dreams were showing me who I *was* (or was in danger of *becoming*)—someone who is dissatisfied with where he is, but who is also too *scared* to ever risk venturing onward and leaving it all behind. All dreams show us who we *are*, and even those first dreams—the ones that I never want to wake up from—are perhaps nothing more than *warnings*, for me, against being the person who (all too often) I know that I am: someone who falls too quickly (and too *fully*) in love with *dreams*—seduced by the safety of unreal *illusions*—in place of trying to love out in the real world, where everything is so much more difficult and *imperfect*.

One of my most continually relevant dreams came to me a week or two after I returned home, having lived the past five months in Paris. To quote the first sentence of the description that I wrote of it—"*I fell in love with France...I meant to write,* in France..." I didn't meet anyone in France, in that sense; that's not (really) what it's about. My dream, though, was all about falling in love with a young French woman. She was blonde and beautiful, the sort of effervescent, indescribable *beauty* that you can only ever find in *dreams*. The whole movement of the dream was about spending so much time with this young girl and letting myself become foolish and *happy*, not holding myself erect and *detached* all the time. But—for most of the dream—I didn't think I loved her. I knew that she loved *me*, and I was painfully weary of causing her pain—because, all too soon, I would be *leaving*. That was the sense of *foolishness* I felt in the dream: to fall in love—to get so close to someone—when you're destined to *leave* them, so soon. For most of the dream, I thought that her foolishness was to fall in love with *me*, while mine was rather the foolishness of letting her fall for me so *forcefully*, when I was all too aware of the pain that it would soon (inevitably) cause her.

Then, at the end of the dream, I'm sitting somewhere—talking to someone about my time in France—from which I've just come *back*. Naturally, I tell him about this girl, whom I didn't *love*, but who was so *wonderful*, and with whom I shared such beautiful moments. When I'm done, he says—reflectively—that it seems as if I really *did* love her. Tears are still coming to my eyes as I write this, now—for the *dream*, and for everything it *signifies*. Because—in this instant—I realize that I really *had* loved her, I just couldn't admit it to myself. I was trying to save *myself* from the pain of leaving, just as much as I was trying to save *her*. I held myself back from loving more (or, at least, from *admitting* that love) because it was myself—just as much, if not more, than her—who I was trying to protect from feeling *too much* when (all too soon) it *ended*.

The dream showed me to myself in the form of a *self-portrait*, as I was and have so often been. I did not fall in love with a beautiful young French girl during my time in Paris, but I did fall in *love*—with the city, with the country, with my life there, with life *everywhere*. The sort of *love* that you feel when you truly are content to be where you are, and to live as you do. When you find yourself opening up to new *experiences*, to other *people*, to *Life*, itself. (In other words: when you feel at *home*...) I felt myself opening up in France—I felt myself falling in love—in a way that I hadn't done in so many years. And, once I came back from France, it was this *dream*—lingering in my thoughts, *pricking* me every time I thought of it—which inspired me to do *better*, and to be more *honest*, should the opportunity for love ever come to me again. It would take four months (lived life, after all, moves so much slower than the realizations we have of it), but when love did come again, I felt more open and more ready to *run* after it, than I had been before. (*You ran after me that first night*...)

Occasionally, words or phrases—including the title of this book—also come to me in dreams. *And I washed myself with words*...That line came to me many years ago, clamping down on my soul so *forcefully* that—when I woke up—I attempted to make a poem out of it. I wrote a few stanzas, but (like most of my works of fiction) it never totally *clicked*, and I left it—unfinished—not long after. *And I washed myself with words*...How did that apply to me? What deep-seated truth did it reveal, more concisely and imaginatively—and more *correctively*—than I could ever have put it in waking life? The (unfinished) poem had been about a young girl in the shower, trying—with words—to wash off a harsh sexual experience. (Perhaps her first time, to someone who left her in a bad *place*...) Which is to say—life, at that time, felt like an *uncomfortable* experience, for me. Instead of dealing with things (in a reasonable amount of time) and then moving on with life, I would retreat to a solitary room— either with a computer, or a pad and pen—and instead soothe myself with *words*. Washing off the accumulated dirt of *reality*—and the pain of *experience*—through the purifying act of writing. Or, as I would later put it (in a sort of love letter): being held back by my own *"reticence too great for life,"* a reticence which had only ever inspired—in place of *real* affection—*"a flurry of belatedly-beautiful words..."*

For the longest time, I thought that *Circumambulate*—that unforgettable dream-word— was less a *corrective*, than an exceptional, divine *gift*, bestowed (by the gods!) upon a poor, slumbering mortal. (*Cir-cum-am-bu-late*—one of those five-syllable words that would have *fascinated* me in spelling class in second grade...) I hadn't remembered seeing it before, and—at first—I didn't even think it was a real *word*. But *circumambulate* was *real* ("*To walk around in a circle...*"), and—even though it sounded *strange* to my ears—it also felt so *meaningful*. ("*To walk all the way around (something)...*") Soon enough, *circumambulate* became the catalyst that finally drove me to *write*, as I had always believed—and always doubted—I was *able* to write. ("*To walk around (something), especially ceremoniously...*") It became the sort of central *point*, around which so many ideas—all circling in my head—finally came harmoniously *together*. ("*To circle on foot, especially as part of a ritual...*")

In other words, I had seemingly forgotten my own understandings of dreams, and how they show me what I am, not as something to seek or to strive *towards*, but rather as something to be warned against and *corrected*. It was only after two months that I finally came to question what *circumambulate* meant to me, and to doubt the very *dream* from which it sprang. What if *circumambulate* carried instead that simpler, more blunt meaning—"*to avoid the point*"—which I had always been aware of, but didn't give foremost importance? What if *circumambulate*—as a reflection of myself—just showed me talking around and around in circles, but never actually *saying* anything? What if the truth of the dream was that all my thoughts and writing were just *repeating* and *repeating*, completely avoiding the *point*? What if I were just circling and circling around *myself*—

never really seeing myself *honestly*—at all? Either my interpretation of my dreams—as *correctives*—was incomplete, or I had fallen into that trap that my dreams always (inadvertently?) set for me.

Ultimately, I think I agree with Freud's understanding of dreams as *wish-fulfillment*, but for the *interpretation* of the dream, and not for the dream itself. To quote Jorge Luis Borges (paraphrasing Samuel Taylor Coleridge): *"In our dreams...images represent the sensations we think they cause; we do not feel horror because we are threatened by a sphinx; we dream of a sphinx in order to explain the horror we feel..."* In other words, though we may dream of our family or friends, our dreams do not really tell us anything about *them*—they only speak to *us*, and what *we* are feeling. The word *"circumambulate"* comes to me in a dream, not because I *want* to be going around in a circle, but because I already *am*. Yet, it is still up to *us*—the ones who remember our dreams, and who try to *understand*—to figure out what they mean: whether what they show us is *good* or *bad*, something to be *sought* out or *avoided*. For—in the end—it is not our dreams that judge for *us*, but we who judge our *dreams*.

12.14.07, 10.06.07

In my younger days, I was precipitated more towards *provocation* than I am now. I was doing a presentation in front of the class (on Existentialism, of course!), filled with excessively long, pompous, impassioned, and philosophically-immature declamations about *Freedom*, *Nothingness*, and all those other sorts of *deep* and *profound* subjects that high school students always seem to be thinking about. I had the brilliant idea to write a personalized question for everyone in the class, ranging from things like *"Who are you?"* and *"What does it mean to be a human?"* to *"Is suicide always just a way out?"* and *"Can people ever be truly happy?"* I also had the audacity to think that I knew each of these persons well enough (perhaps better than they knew themselves!) to challenge them in the most bitter and fundamental way possible, according to how I thought they could most *grow* as individuals.

There was one young woman, in particular, whose question I rewrote—*literally*—at least twenty times. I really didn't know anything about her (aside from the fact that she, her sister, and her mother often went grocery shopping on Sunday mornings), and—to this day—I still don't really know anything about her. The only meaningful thing I knew of her life was that something had happened in her past, which had seemingly *changed* everything. I could speculate what it was (then and now), but the only things clear were that she thought about it every single day, and not in a *painless* way. That someone— whether intentionally, or not—had *hurt* her, deeply. I didn't know her, and she didn't know me, and yet I asked (wrote) one of the most *inappropriate* things I have ever expressed in my life, to someone who was (at best) a friendly acquaintance:

> *"Does the past lose its value because it no longer exists and doesn't connect with the present?"*

(Did I believe that, when I wrote it? Not really. But I did know all too well the danger of the contrary extreme—the inability to acknowledge the past as *passed*. I knew all too well—personally—the need to be pushed back into inhabiting the *present*, not forgetting the past but also no longer being *consumed* by it...)

I overheard—once my presentation had ended, and all my questions had been asked and answered— that she was (rightly, understandably) *furious* with me. (I'm still sort of furious with *myself*, to be honest...) But that's both the power and the folly of youth—to boldly dare things about which one is so *impassioned* and *certain*. Immediately afterwards, though, I regretted it. The rest of the day, my stomach was twisted in knots. I could barely eat, fearing (but also—strangely—*hoping*) that she might talk to me later, and make me face what I had done.

(The moral of the story?) She did walk up to me, later in the day. And—in a strange way—it seemed as if she was *thanking* me. She certainly never said the words "*thank*" and "*you*" together, which might have implied that what I had done was either laudable or faultless. Yet, the very fact that she was talking to me now (without *anger*, when it might have made more sense for her to be *screaming* at me!), seemed to imply a sort of understanding— maybe even *appreciation*—of what I had done.

I have an excellent memory for feelings and ideas, but not for specific words. So—though I don't remember *what* she said to me—I do remember the *sentiment*. It's like she was surprised. Like she found it strange—*unexpected*—that I had paid so much attention, as to be able to ask such a piercing question. (*You listen really well...*) I told her—in the smallest voice, almost stuttering—that I had really tried to listen to the personal speeches that everyone in the class had given earlier in the year.

When I began writing the questions for my presentation, I thought back to those speeches, and three of them stuck out to me. "*If everything is egotistical, then isn't it the same as if nothing were egotistical?*" went to someone who—during their speech—had seemed profoundly dismayed over the unavoidable, intolerable idea that every single thing that anyone ever did in the world was *selfish*. "*Are we all hopelessly alone?*" went to the person who had talked about the elemental power of *friendship*, and who—I could sense (like finds like!)—had already known the pain of *solitude* in her life. Then there was that question about the valuelessness of the *past*, which I knew would cause the strongest reaction, but which I also felt I *most* had to write. That question went to her, this young woman who was now standing in front of me, talking to me, and who—for the length of a sentence, at least—I felt as if I *knew*, without ever having known her…

I haven't talked to her in many years, and it's unlikely that I'll ever talk to her again. I hope she knows that I'm sorry, but that I also would have done it again. I hope she knows that the question was something I could only ask, having lived through the bitter thought of it *myself*. That, with the question, I wanted to hold up a darkly honest and piercingly blunt mirror in which to see yourself, to question your own existence, and—if called to—to find a better way to *live*. The question still works as a mirror for me, in those times when I still forget (after all these years!) the easily forgotten lesson that it challenges us to learn.

01.15.12, 01.21.12

Something strange happens when you're unquestionably in *love*, or when you've undertaken a gargantuan, time-starved *project*—you find yourself saying things that mean so much more than you realize...

Like most college students, I had acquired the terrible habit of *procrastination*, a condition which had only worsened over the years. It should be no surprise, then, that—seven semesters in, and with one more to go—I found myself standing before an impossible task: to write 70 pages of a senior philosophy thesis in five days. Of course, I didn't *know* it would be 70 pages, at the time. The minimum was 25, but I had a depressingly confident feeling that—in order to say everything I wanted to say—mine would end up significantly *longer*.

I basically didn't talk to anyone during those five days. And—when I did—at least half of my mind wasn't really there, still endlessly circling around my *thesis*. I couldn't carry on a conversation of more than a few minutes. I saw the whole world as if through a *veil*, beyond which nothing seemed as real or as important as what was going on in my own head, and how that translated into my *thesis*. I went to all my classes, and even went to my job, but so much of my life was spent—either in the library, or in my bedroom—*writing*. I hardly ate anything, because I couldn't risk diverting more than the absolute minimum of energy (that energy so vital to *creation*) to digestion. That week, I slept at most four or five hours a night— oftentimes, more like two or three. I got into the habit of letting myself sleep (or, more accurately, simply lying down) for an hour or half-hour, anytime that I started to yawn, or my focus began to slip. I stayed up most of the night, and woke up early each morning to write. I depended on *music* to survive, nourished wholly by the energy—and the rhythm—of the songs. (The more *spare* and *heartbroken* the music, the better...)

I knew I was somewhat *crazy* that week. But I also knew that I *had* to be crazy, in order to write my thesis—and not just because of the foolishly impossible situation into which I had placed myself. That's something I've always known, but didn't admit until recently: in order to write—to write, *anything*—I need to become a little bit *crazy*. Since high school, every paper I wrote—without exception—had been written with *music* playing in the background. I had needed to block out the rest of the world—surrounding myself, on all sides, by *sound*—in order to fully enter the subject I was writing about, and to throw myself into the world of my own *words*. Writing, after all (at least for me), requires a different sort of *concentration* than the one we bring to other aspects of our lives. It demands an honesty and an accessibility to the deepest, most *obscure* regions of ourselves, which, most of the time, we keep *hidden*—whether because they're in some way *incompatible* with the everyday world, or perhaps because we, ourselves, can't bear to *see* (or to *deal* with) what they might reveal.

Seven days before the due date, I only had ten rough pages of my thesis finished. It took me two days of being wracked by anxiety—utterly *paralyzed* before the page—in order to finally begin to write. Part of it was the self-accusation I continually (and rightly) subjected myself to, lamenting the impossible *plight* I found myself in, and berating *myself* for being the one who had brought me there. Part of it, too, was simply my *fear* before the written word. (Over the years, the more I had *read*, the more I had realized how little I—*myself*—had to say...) I essentially shut down—not writing, not doing anything, except oscillating between *fear* and *self-anger*—for two whole days. Eventually, though, *something* won out. Suddenly, it was like I found myself in a sort of *tunnel* vision, completely enveloped by a consummate *attention* on the task. I felt some other, *deeper* power pulsing through me (as if my *animal* instincts were taking over), and—somehow—letters became words, words turned into sentences, and an entire, 70-page *whole* eventually came from all these small, individual *parts*.

Anyway, I finished it, but not without a frantic and *crazed* rush at the deadline, followed by a sort of total, complete *numbness*, afterwards. I didn't know if it was *good* or not, and—to be honest—I didn't even *care*. At some point, any judgment about whether something was *good* or *bad*, *true* or *false*, *valuable* or *worthless*, flew out the window, along with any and all *hesitation* on my part. I was still a writer, of course—choosing words, forming sentences, and deciding how I wanted them to sound. But my writing was no longer guided by what was good or not, by what was true or not, but simply and wholly by what sounded—what *felt*—true to my ears. I've always written by the feel of the phrases, following the internal *rhythm* that they formed in my head. For my thesis, though, there was *only* the rhythm of the words (echoing off the rhythm of the music in the background) to guide my writing, keeping me on that path of unstoppable forward momentum which—moving from small part to small part—eventually achieved something immense and *great*, even though I knew it might not be *good*.

The subject of my thesis—a rewriting of one of the best papers I had written at college— was the way that Friedrich Nietzsche[1] approached the idea of the "*self*" or the "*soul*" throughout his works. Nietzsche's aim (as I understood it this time around) had been to *critique* and then to *reevaluate* the notion of the "*self*"—along with other, related notions—in order to replace the *unhealthy* ideas we currently hold for ones which are *healthier* and ultimately more *joyous* to life. (*You give me philosophy lessons even though I don't understand half of them...*) The truth, though, is that I wasn't really writing about *Nietzsche*. Or—if I was—then I wasn't writing about him in the way that a *philosopher* would. A philosopher *presents* ideas, *comments* on them, *critiques* them, *defends* them, *expands* them, and—simply—tries to *understand* them. In my thesis, though, what I tried (unknowingly) to do was to have Nietzsche *face* Nietzsche—to have Nietzsche interrogate *himself*—in order to see what (if anything) came out of it. As if what I tried to express in my thesis were not his *ideas*, but he *himself*—the individual Friedrich Nietzsche—as he once might have thought and *lived* those ideas. As

1 Famous German philosopher of the 19th century, known primarily (and, perhaps, misguidedly) for the infamous statement that "God is dead"; for the supposed connection between his works and anti-Semitism and National Socialism; and for the mental breakdown he experienced in 1889, followed by the silent "madness" in which he spent the last ten years of his life.

if Nietzsche was more like the *language* in which I was writing, than the *subject* about which my thesis was revolving. As if I had been learning that language (steadfastly) for four years, and it was only then—while writing my thesis, during that crazy week—that I had finally reached *fluency,* speaking in the *language* of Nietzsche but only to talk about a completely *different* subject.

The week I wrote my thesis was also the first week of classes, all of which I attended in my crazed, half-aware state. As I was writing, there had been moments—something which I'm sure all writers know—when I found myself *surprised* by the things I was writing. As if the ideas and sentences appearing before me on the page were things that (in my circumscribed, deeply repetitive life) I had never *thought* before. I experienced several of these moments as I wrote my thesis, but I was always too pressed for time to give them more than an "*Aha!*" and a slight tilt of the head, before moving on to the next phrase. Sitting in my last class of the week, though (half of my attention elsewhere), I was suddenly visited by sentences—utterly *surprising* sentences—like they come to me in *dreams.* (*Greatness won't get you to any beyond...*[2]) Sentences which did not come from *me*—which were not in *my* voice—but which struck me to the

2 Or, as it would be refined by memory—*Neither greatness nor love will get you to any beyond...*

core, nonetheless. (*Let yourself go, let life express itself; it will make you happier now, and it will let you see yourself more clearly later...*) They were sentences that had almost nothing to do with the class I was in, and—astonishingly—also seemed to have little to do with my *thesis*, either. (*It is a heavy clarity with which I now see (the weight of the no-beyond)...*) Even the ones that seemingly employed Nietzschean terminology or concepts (*Love as the fullest expression of the will-to-power, life going beyond itself...*) weren't really speaking about a 19th century German philosopher, but about something smaller, more acute, and—ultimately—something more *personal*. (*Going beyond, but never getting there...*)

I hardly thought about myself during those five days. Or (perhaps more accurately)I hardly thought about myself during those five days, in comparison to the tremendous vanity and *self-absorption* with which I normally spend time—each day—reflecting on myself. Or (perhaps *most* honestly), I spent five days continually, *incessantly* thinking about myself—having put on the outer garments of Herr Nietzsche—in the guise of my *thesis*. For me, part of the craziness of writing comes from being so much more *honest* with myself—more focused on myself, in a far different way—than I normally am. I will spend hours looking at myself, but, most of the time (I hate to admit it), I never get beyond a *surface* investigation—never really avoid the bias and *need* that obscures all self-reflection, never really see into the *depths* of what I truly am. It was only here—writing my thesis, and seemingly not looking for them, at all—that some of the strongest and clearest self-realizations finally came to me, *unbidden* but not *unneeded*. (*Greatness won't get you to any beyond…*) That line, especially, struck me—like a bolt of *lightning*—and for ten minutes I ignored the class I was in, I ignored the thesis I was writing, and simply thought about how deeply, *fundamentally* that sentence spoke about me and my own life: what I—myself—was, and what I (mistakenly) *thought* I was. Then—once again—I turned my attention outward, because I still had an hour of class (and thirty more hours of writing) ahead of me, before I could loosen my focus and once again face this *reflection* of myself.

To say that these sentences had nothing to do with Nietzsche is to ignore what he—what *any*—work can do for us. Later on, I would form a five-word phrase to sum up what—for me—was the essence of Nietzsche's thought and life: *a challenge to be joyous*. To fully *live* life and to *love* it, both despite and because of all the experience—*painful*, as well as *joyful*—that we will have in this world. And not (as Nietzsche so vehemently argues) to get lost in *ethereal* or *otherworldly* ideas which, all too often, only serve to shield us from having to confront the painful and joyous—the all too *real*—reality of our lives. In other words (and this is only what I realized after), to remember that *greatness*[3] won't get you to any *beyond*. That hoping the attainment of *greatness*[4] will rescue you from this life—revealing this world and all its difficulties to be merely a *dream*—only stops us from moving forward to meet life and to greet it *warmly*, as Nietzsche would have urged all of us to do. My thesis was like the process of teaching me a lesson—using the rich and deep language that Nietzsche (both thought and figure) provided—and trying to drive that lesson home again and again, word after word, for 22,000 words, until it finally *stuck*. (*Stuck*, at least, in the paper I had written, if not—*permanently*—in my heart...)

The next day—after I had handed my thesis in—I sat down to write some leftover thoughts (on Nietzsche?) that were lingering in my head: *As if, I want to ask, where has all that pain gone in his life? Does he have pain, or does he refuse to write about that pain? Wandering around Europe, lonely as a fool, who looks into the truth of things and somehow finds a way to rejoice, continually, eternally. And...* The sentence broke off there, because I had suddenly—inexplicably—found myself *bawling*. I almost never cried: my face was too stoic—my composure too

---

3 And *love?*

4 Or *love?*

restrained and self-aware—to simply let myself *go* in that way. In the past five years, I had only cried four times—watching *The Pianist*, one of my last days in high school; hearing of the death of a former classmate; after a break-up; and a couple months earlier, when I was saying goodbye to something that had been a central part of my life the past four years. Now, sitting in my room, before my computer—as I had been so much the past week—I was *crying*, and seemingly for no reason. (There was a reason, but it would take me awhile to *see* it, through the newly emerging pattern of those tears...) It felt like I just needed to break down, to tear off my entire veneer of stoicism—*to let myself go*—and to open myself up to what I was *feeling*, even if that meant sobbing (pathetically) into my hands.

At the time, it was probably physical and spiritual *exhaustion*, as much as anything else. After being so crazed and vulnerable, I not-infrequently fall *sick* at the end of a particularly insightful essay. This time seemed different, though—it seemed *more*. That makes sense, since my thesis was the longest thing I had ever written in my life, and—in its own way—perhaps also the *truest*. After my tears slowed down, and then finally stopped, I went on to write (unsurprisingly) eighteen pages of philosophical, critical prose, with only scattered mentions here and there of anything even remotely *personal*. (The deeper, *unwritten* truth of those pages, though?) I had undergone a sort of *change*, one which was bringing me back to the world—the vale—of tears, from which I had exempted myself (except for a few, acute events), over the past nine years. It had always been *death* or *love* (or—more accurately—the *death of love*) that brought me to tears. Then what sort of *death*—and what sort of *love*—was causing my tears, now?

Life, over time, with language and thought, tends to solidify, to congeal—the stream of life tends to slow down, become viscous, perhaps even freeze (the winter of life)...I had finally admitted—and buried—my hopes for a dreamlike, transcendental *beyond*, which had carried me through so many winters, and which will probably (in the future) carry me through many more. The Spring was coming, when I would finally thaw out and love again. Maybe that's what my tears really were: the running over of a newly flowing *river*, one which would no longer be frozen and contained in itself, but could break down and overflow as it followed the inevitable currents— up and down—of *life*. That, at least, is how I had always understood Kafka's famous line: "*A book must be the axe for the frozen sea within us*," opening us up—*violently*, if necessary—to the flow of *life*, and *reality*, and *pain*, and *joy*, from which (all too often) we have closed ourselves off. The act of reading (*books*, or *ourselves*) is so taxing—so full of *feeling*—that we can't just step out of it, easily or painlessly. And perhaps we shouldn't want to, either, since that suffering may be the price we have to pay for the *openness* which such reading can inspire in us. Maybe we need to become sick, or go crazy, or break down into tears, or feel emptied, in order for a book to do what it aims to do. But then (as Nietzsche would say), maybe we first need to get *sicker*, in order to get *better*.

05.12.12, 12.19.11

The best date I ever planned took place at the end of the year—the last night we would be together—before she left campus, and I (a few days later) would graduate...

The date was a mix of several different things: the grand, sentimental (and *legendary*) schemes that you find on television shows; an over-active memory (one that remembers more than *most* people do); and my own penchant for grand journeys through space and time, treating every small detail as if it were a *sign* sent by the universe. The plan was to walk around campus, revisiting all the special places—reliving all the special moments—that we had shared together, during the past two months. There was food (*3.22, 3.25*), photos (*3.26, 4.20, 5.3*), music (*3.24*), and videos (*3.23, 4.29*), as well as chances to play sports (*4.14, 5.1*) and to read scenes from a play (*4.16*), all designed to take us back—in *time*, and in *space*—to those two months we had been together. The date began where our relationship had begun (*3.19*), and it ended in the present moment (*5.12*)—standing *where* and *when* we were—but also sealed with a promise (*a book, a letter*) that we would be together in the present to come.

Thinking back on it—even now—it has always seemed to *sparkle* in my memory, like it was so much more than a date, albeit a magical one. *(3.19— That first night, when we went waterfalling, talked for hours, and then departed, with a hug—but I ran after her, because I also wanted to kiss her goodnight...)* It was like we were playing ourselves in the drama— comedy or tragedy?—of our *relationship*, as it had been written the past two months. *(4.1—The day we officially started going out, and how awkward it was...)* It was like we were figures walking through a landscape painting, passing not just through space but also *time*, remembering a different moment with each brushstroke. *(4.4—The time I needed her, and she came without question...)* It was like we had rewound the film of our *love*, and were now replaying it for ourselves—as spectators—to see. *(4.5—The time I surprised her, trying to cheer her up at the end of a bad day...)* It was like a realm of shared nostalgia, where our memories flowed through each other and we could revisit them *together*. *(5.1—Our one-month anniversary, which we celebrated only because we knew we wouldn't have too many more of them...)* The date was all of these things, and so many more *metaphors* and *symbols* that I could make up to describe it. *(5.4— The first time we said I love you...)* But what was it really? *(You plan the BEST things...)* A poor, love-struck, overly-sensitive person's vain attempt to keep alive a past that he had *loved* so much, and that he knew would *fade*, all too soon...

§

My refrain, at that time—and the theme of that entire date I planned—was that *Everything is eternal*. It was a sort of willful misreading of Nietzsche's idea of the Eternal Return[5], but—for me—this eternity applied to *memory*, rather than to *reality*. As if there was an *eternity* to everything, because everything—no matter how *grand* or *small*—leaves a mark on the *universe*, which itself is eternal and unforgetting. As if no moment ever disappeared or faded away, because every moment still existed— fully, *unchanged*—in the perfect *memory* of the universe. I probably couldn't have gotten through the two months before, if I hadn't had that idea to *console* others—and to console *myself*. But I also couldn't help thinking (*lamenting*)—*If only I had such a perfect memory! If only others did, too!*

§

There were 27 stops on our date, each one corresponding to a different *date* on the calendar. That meant we had had 27 *memorable* days— sometimes with multiple events on each day—within the 55 days that we had been *together*. (I excluded all those moments from the first four months—when we had merely loved each other *silently*, and from *afar*—because that would've stretched the date to hours, if not *days*...) For me, I have always felt a

---

5 That everything in the universe repeats and will repeat—exactly the same, over and over—for all *eternity*...

special connection to the *date* on the calendar. I remember so many moments of my life, and—when I think back on them—it's so often the date (*February 21*, *May 29*, *August 6*) that stands out as the *symbol* of everything I once experienced. And not only the date, but—so often—the *day* (*Friday, October 30*, *Monday, March 19*), as well. As if—together—that combination of *date* and *day* formed a special code or key (*Friday, February 19*, *Sunday, September 23*), one which gives me the *fullest* access to the *deepest* parts of my memory...

A year later, though—when the calendar has almost completed a full *revolution*, and the anniversary of a significant moment is coming up—I find myself having a *visceral* connection to the past. I can't turn my thoughts *away* from that time; I start entering into the same *mood* that I felt, then; and—almost always—I find myself *emptied* by the thought of how much *time* has passed, how much *life* has already slipped through my fingertips, and how *unrecoverable*—how *unreal*—that moment, now is. Because, a year later—when the anniversary of a memorable moment *does* come back—it's never quite the *same*. The *date* on the calendar may be the same, but the *day* is always different: *Monday, August 10*, becomes *Tuesday, August 10th*; *June 6*—a *Wednesday*—instead becomes a *Friday*; and that special *code*—that vital *key* to the past—disappears, taking along with it an essential part of the *memory* itself. Time slowly distances *everything* from us. Or—maybe—it's that time slowly distances *us* from everything. (Or—maybe the truest—time slowly distances us from *ourselves*...) It's the same for the anniversaries of the *happiest* moments, as well as the *saddest*. If anything, it's *worse* for the happiest ones, because then I am all the more aware of what I have lost, and what is so difficult— perhaps *impossible*—to ever find, again...

Most of the moments, though, that mean something to us—that we *want* to hold onto— are *shared*. Anyone who has ever been taken by nostalgia knows how much more *powerful* a memory is, when it belongs to another person, as well. (Or—at least—when we *think* it is...) Love *is* what it is, because it is shared. Love *was* what it was, because it still lives on in both the memories of those who (once) shared it. But memories *fade*, and *people* forget, and one loves replaces *another*, until it's only a faint—perhaps *sweet*, perhaps *bitter*, but undoubtedly *altered*—feeling that we now have, of a once-begotten *love*. But to love again—to move *on*— don't we have to forget (in a not insignificant way) the love that *was*, but no longer *is*? Don't I *have* to forget—and doesn't the *other* have to forget—until finally the memory has lost all sense of once being *shared*, and of once being *love*, at all?

Me, at the time of our date—in the middle of our love—I couldn't *handle* this thought. I strove with all my being to *cement* these memories—to tangibly *recreate* these moments we had shared—so that our love would not fade with the passage of time or the dwindling of our recollections. If the date—ultimately—was *romantic*, then it's just as true to say that it was *pitiful*. If it was *beautiful*, then it's also necessary to call it *tragic*. If it was all designed for *her*, then (if one is going to be *honest*) it was also designed for *me*, to keep alive in both of us the *love* that I selfishly could not bear to lose—could not bear the thought of it one day being engulfed by an overriding and merciless *present*. This present—*here*—we were together, and it was *perfect*; but another present—not too far into the future—it would be like none of this had ever *happened*. Or, like it hadn't meant as much as we *thought* it did. Or, like we no longer thought of it as *love*, just a passing *fancy*. At another moment—not too far in the future—we may have found ourselves doubting whether the other person ever really *loved* us—or whether we ever really loved *them*—at all. One day, we may have found ourselves looking back on it all with *spite*, or *anger*, or *bitterness*, or with some emotion other than that *love* which we once felt—so powerfully—*together.*

Several months later (when it was ending), I tearfully confessed this impossible *fear* to her. It seems like we cried about anything even *remotely* personal, at that time. (Or at least I did). But this was sharper, different, *deeper*: I knew that she would *forget* me—not tomorrow, not in a few weeks, maybe not even in a *year*—but, one day, she would forget *me*, and forget *us*, and forget all that our *love* once was. (And me, would I forget *her*?) That inevitable *forgetting* is a simple truth, one that I've already learned—so many times—in my life. But, like a child, I still hollered and carried on—still wouldn't *accept*—this simple, unavoidable *fact*: that this was the way things (always) were...

§

At the end of our date—thanks to a good friend's suggestion—I wanted to give her something to symbolize that all this was not just in the *past*, but in the *future*, as well. Six months earlier—at the beginning of what I would later call my *mental courtship*—I had written a sort of essay, inspired by a line of Kurt Vonnegut's: "*Of all the words of mice and men, the saddest are 'It might have been'*"... For me— both at the time of writing that essay, and now— there are few sentiments more *beautiful* than that one. And, long ago—back in December, when I first started loving her—that *beauty* had inspired me to imagine *what might have been* between us, she and I, if we were ever to have a real *relationship*. (*The first time we ever talked, us two, alone, and how awkward it would have been...*) It was—essentially—a personal piece, full of my own past, history, and feelings *(And I would start putting too much faith in my dreams...),* but one that always came back to the idea—seemingly unlikely, at the time—of her and me *together. (And all the TV shows that she would try, and succeed, to get me to watch; and all the books I would suggest to her to read, without expecting any of them to be enjoyed or liked by her...)* Later on—after she read had it—she would also be amazed at how *prophetic* the essay had turned out to be. (*And those fears and worries that she had that I would try to comfort her for; and those fears that I would, slowly, come to admit...*)

Ultimately, though, if it's true to call the sentiment of that letter *beautiful*, then it's just as true to say that it was *painful*. (*And if it were to last some weeks, some months, what then?*) If the sentiment's *sweet*, that's only because it's *bittersweet*. (*Would it end happily, or in anger and sadness?*) For what I had ended up writing was the most beautiful *dream* of us—together—that I could imagine, overflowing with my love of her. (*And I might try and write things for her, which I'd have to explain as being inspired by her in a deeper way than if I had merely written about her...*) The essay was proof of how *much*—and for how *long*—I had loved her, yes.

(*For myself, to let things change and adapt, and not to be afraid to be a Nietzschean and in love…*) But, when I wrote it, the essay had only been that—a *dream*—and nothing more. (*For myself, my own fight not to think about the future, and not to plan ahead more than a few weeks…*) Because, ultimately, the person who wrote that essay never would have said anything—to her—at *all*. (*Another girl who I was too scared to actually pursue, one of the first which I actually, in a weak sense, did pursue…*) Because—if it had been up to that person—*nothing* ever would have come of it, their relationship never would have *happened*, and they never would have been sharing that *moment*, on that *date*, looking back on what a bittersweet essay that *he*—that *I*—had once written. (*And how it might have just ended at that, with nothing more, except a silent and unsent letter, to myself, about everything I imagined would happen if I were to ever say anything to her…*)

At the end of our date—when I handed her this essay—I had turned it into a *letter*, something I had never imagined doing when I first wrote it. In some sense, it always had been a letter, but one that I had written to *myself*—to be read, sometime in the future—in order to see what, if anything, ever came of all that *love* I felt for her. (*And I will look back on this document and laugh, sadly and with joy, that once upon a time I imagined thus, so much wrong and so much right...)* But, I realized, I *had* to give her this essay—I had to turn it into a letter, to someone *else*—in order to dare to make this beautiful *dream* into a *reality*, and to challenge the very *sentiment* from which the whole essay had sprung. *(So naïve and so at all beginning, so aware of the bitterness and the desire to avoid it all, so scared to actually do anything about it beyond the joy of the secret courtship...)* For, in that moment, we could both read through the essay—seeing just how *prophetic* it all had been— only because *(so much right)* it expressed that deep and lasting *love* that I had for her, but also because *(so much wrong)* its author had been too *scared* to do anything more than to write about it, long ago, in an essay...

Ultimately, I had to confront and go through my own *past* (in that letter, on our date) in order to see what sort of *beauty* all of those things held, and to see—that moment in May—what sort of *love* they all symbolized. Was it the beauty of *dreams*, always tinged with the sad smile of regret—regret over *what might have been* between us; or regret over what *had* been, but *was*, no longer? Or was it the beauty of foreshadowing *(so much wrong and so much right)* what had actually been *shared*, between us—and what would *continue* to be shared, between us—in *reality*? In the end, I had needed to share with her all of these things from my *past,* in order for us—*both* of us—to see not only how much I *had* loved her, but how much I would *continue* to love her, as well. Giving her the letter at the end of the date was like a *symbol* of how much I had grown: how (at my best) I had learned to look on the *past* not as something to be *regretted* or *longed* for, but rather as the continual inspiration to do *better*—and to *love* someone—both *now* and *later*. At its best, the past became for me not only a means to improve myself in the *present*, but a *promise* that I would strive for the same, in the present to come—in the *future*, when we would still be together...

11.14.11, 04.15.12

Probably the most significant thing I did during my four years of college was to play on the school's Quidditch team...

For as far back as I can remember (and probably before that, too), I've always been *competitive*. Whether it was organized sports, or friendly card games, or even (*especially*) grades in school, I've always needed to *win*, to be the *best*. When I was younger—and sometimes, too, when I was older—I would (not infrequently) end up complaining, or yelling, or *crying*, if I ever suffered the unbearable agony of *losing*. (As some people—perhaps more accurately—would put it: *I've always been* extremely *competitive...*)

And yet—even for all my competitiveness—I didn't play a *normal* sport, in college. I chose to play Quidditch: a sport that was born in the most *unserious* way possible—adapted from a children's book about wizards and witches—and one which was (self-consciously) *silly*, infused with the *whimsy* of Snitches and the *foolishness* of running around with a broom between your legs. (Alas, we don't fly—at least not yet!) And yet, even for all its childishness and absurdity, Quidditch is still—truly—a *sport*: rather physically demanding, requiring skill and strategy, with an official rulebook, referees, scheduled matches, and large, multi-day tournaments. (When I was a captain, I was always trying to make the team *better*, whether that meant doing *drills*, running *suicides*, or even—not infrequently—*screaming* at someone, when they made a mistake...) In other words, Quidditch was the perfect sport for someone like *me*, who could both dedicate himself to becoming the *best* Quidditch player in the world, but who also needed (oh so badly!) a sense of carelessness, fun, and *levity*, in his life...

(Stay good, run a lot, do lots of drills, do lots of conditioning early—you'll be thankful for it later—practice at least 3 times a week, have lots of social events early on—especially for the freshmen—have lots of games/ tournaments early on if possible, to get that intenser bonding experience...)

Quidditch—in its own way—was at the *center* of my life, throughout college. I gave it so much of my time, my energy, my attention, and (to be honest) my *love*, during those four years. It was as if my entire college experience had been defined by this one activity, and everything that I went through—all the things (great and terrible) that happened during those *oh-so-formative* years—ultimately centered on this club, and on all the *people* who were in it...

(Above all, this is something I've realized: your role as a captain seems to me to make the experience of Quidditch— and through it the entire year/college experience— memorable, and to give lots of points on the path of life that you can look back on fondly and think about...)

Every year—for the past seven years—a Quidditch World Cup has been held. The last year I participated, there were over 100 teams—from the United States, as well as Canada and Europe—and the tournament was held on a giant sports complex in New York City. (Rather different from my first World Cup—four years earlier—which had only 12 teams, and took place on a muddy, college campus in Vermont…) The World Cup was always a significant—and memorable—moment in my life. Though the dates would change, it was always in the Fall (my favorite season). Though my team changed from year to year, we always did well, especially the two years we finished 2nd (out of 12 teams) and 4th (out of 50). And—each year—my experience at the World Cup ultimately led me to a sort of *climax* in my life, bringing either deep *insights* (about myself), *love* (real and shared), or the ability to finally get *over* love (once it was gone…)

(Remembering inside jokes, and horrible weather at tournaments, and dumb decisions on the pitch, and all the Facebook photos that you have from it, and all these things take you back to that time in your life, and you loved it all, and you are glad to have loved it and to have been there as you were…)

It wouldn't be going too far to say that the World Cup was the highlight of the year for Quidditch, and—for me—it was often the highlight of *everything*

I experienced, during those twelve months. It gave me something significant to work towards—and to be *excited* about—for weeks and months ahead of time. It demanded so much focus and *energy* on my part that my entire being—*physically*, as well as *mentally*—became concentrated and *heightened*. Then—during the tournament itself—there was all the pleasure and *fun* that I had from it. Whether we were playing well and *winning*, or simply being *silly* with each other, I felt like I was really close to my teammates—like I was finally part of a community, a *family*...

(And I think in that way Quidditch can and does often serve as the prism through which you can experience these 4 years of your life, because it is and can be so time-consuming, but consuming time in such a good way, giving you friends and a family and expectations and goals and work to do—but work that you enjoy—and something to constantly talk about and think about, and a tangible reality with results that you can hold onto...)

The weekend of the World Cup—to put it simply—brought out the *best* in me: I was ready and open for *everything*. It's no coincidence that the seeds of my first *love* were planted that weekend, or that I'd finally get over the *loss* of that love when the World Cup came around, the following year. The same story would repeat at my last World Cup, when I caught the eye of a beautiful freshman and couldn't stop myself from looking towards her, again and again (and *again...*) When it was over—and our team had been eliminated from the last World Cup I would ever play—I went off by myself, to watch the sun set over the New York City skyline. I would be lying if I told you I didn't cry, at that moment. I was crying for everything that I had gotten from this silly, wonderful sport— since that very first day of practice, three years earlier—when I had tried (*oh-so-awkwardly!*) to run around with a broom between my legs. I was crying for everything that I would now be leaving behind—an essential, *vital* part of the past four years of my life, and of everything (both *great* and *terrible*) that had happened during them...

(And I could go on and on, but I hope that you all get a sense of what Quidditch has meant to me: joy in life, time with other people, but also the time spent in solitude thinking about Quidditch and wanting to get better, the pain of bruises and coldness, and the pleasure of all those wonderful things we've done, and the people you meet, and the things you do, and the places you go...)

Five months later—and on the verge of graduating—I played in my very last Quidditch tournament, which our team hosted. As always, I was excessively *competitive*, focusing more than anyone else on *winning* and going out on top. (We won the tournament—and, to be honest, it wasn't even close...) But I also made sure to *enjoy* everything, as much as I could—dying my hair pink (our school color), taking funny photos, and (most importantly) not being afraid to let myself *smile*. It was a good day, and a wonderful way to say goodbye...

(And the long, rambling, Dr. Seuss-quoting essays you write when you're a senior and trying to say goodbye to what has truly been the best thing you could have ever asked for when you came to college—essentially friendless and not quite ready to have friends again—until you found yourself suddenly crying before others, as they talk of the past year you've spent together, and this change coming a mere four years—and countless car rides, hugs, tackles, sleepless nights—later...)

§

The day after that last tournament, though, I was a wreck. When I woke up that morning (Sunday morning, which I usually loved for its peace and solitude), I didn't even want to get out of bed. I was *numb*, and *angry*, and didn't want do *anything*, didn't want to participate in the *world*, in any way. We always had a team dinner on Sundays—something I almost never missed—but I didn't even feel like going to that. (*Especially,* not to that...) During those four years, I had skipped meetings, and lectures I wanted to go to, and even grand events like Convocation, all because I had placed Quidditch above everything—*everything*—else. But now, I didn't want to do *anything*—didn't want talk to *anyone*—that had to do with Quidditch. Eventually—begrudgingly—I walked over to the dining hall, because my girlfriend (who was also on the team) had texted me that I should come. And I knew she was right (or at least part of me did). But I was sullen and unresponsive, probably frowning and silent the entire time I was there...

(Playing Quidditch at midnight, with glow in the dark accessories. All the Scavenger Hunts we did, sending people all over campus, having them complete silly tasks, and rewarding them with wondrously absurd prizes at the end. So many cupcakes and baked goods and bake sales...)

The rest of the afternoon was the same—I was *angry*, *numb*, and *hostile* to the world. I knew I had work that I should have been doing, but I simply couldn't focus—for more than a few moments—without my foul mood getting in the way. I knew that I needed to *write*—to express my feelings and to face what (clearly) I was having trouble dealing with. But getting outside of myself—looking at myself *honestly*—was the last thing in world I wanted to do, at that moment. I was fed up with *everyone*, and *everything*. (Especially *myself,* and my *anger*...) Finally—that night—a moment of lucidity and exasperation came to me. I left my room (for only the second time that day), and walked back towards the Quidditch field, where—for the past four years—I had more or less found my *home*. I didn't know why I was going there: maybe to *cry*, maybe to *scream*, maybe to say *goodbye*—maybe just to *feel* something...

(Parties with Harry Potter-themed food and drink— cakes, butterbeer, chocolate frogs. Disney movie nights. Pond Quidditch. Horcruxes. Dr. Seuss Halloween costumes. 24-hr Read-a-thons. Star-gazing...)

As fate would have it, I passed my girlfriend on the way. I hadn't talked to her since earlier that day, even though I knew I *should* be telling her what I was going through. (That's what you do when you're close to someone, right—admit when you *need* them?) Or, at least, I knew I should be telling her *something*. But whenever that thought came into my head—throughout the day—I *rejected* it, without sympathy or a second thought. Now—suddenly— we were walking towards each other. If I had left a minute earlier, or a minute later, then I never would have had to see her. I didn't *want* to see her, to be honest. And it showed—I was *mean* to her, in a way I had never been before. I wasn't actively, aggressively *nasty*, but I was utterly cold and unfeeling towards her, which (as I knew) was the *cruelest* way I could ever treat her. We talked for a moment or two, but I was terse and scowling, and

I didn't even care. I ignored (chose not to see) the hurt look on her face, as I said goodbye—walking away without a kiss, or a hug, or anything even remotely suggesting *closeness* between us. (And this was the person I was supposed to have loved— madly—the past five months!)

I get mean when I'm leaving something behind. I'm not always the *kindest* or *warmest* person, but it's rare that I am intentionally, outwardly (and unrepentantly) *mean*. My host mother in Paris laughed at it, telling me how *drôle* she found my foul mood. (That's really the best way to take my—occasional—cruelty…) But that's not the way *she* took it—in the moment—when I walked away from her, without so much as a kind word. I knew I had hurt her—and hurt her in the way that few people in the world ever could. We had only been seeing each other a month, but I had long loved her (and had long *known* her), and I knew just how to hurt her the *most*. I knew what I was doing, but I also didn't care. (*You always make me talk and don't just ignore me…*)

Yet—even when I'm a heartless *jerk*—I'm not so blind (or unaware of myself) that I fail to see just how cruel and *unloving* I can be. Nor do I fail to feel—in the slightest sense—*regret* or *guilt* over my unkind actions. After walking a few steps, I stopped, and began turning—around and around (indecisively)—

in circles. I was trying to decide whether I should just *forget* her, and do what I came to do—or whether I should turn around and (once again) run after her. I knew that I *should* go after her, even though I had absolutely no *desire* to do so. I knew (barely) that I am not always a monster, and that—even if I didn't feel it, now—a part of me would *want* to go after her. It was the *best* part of me—perhaps—that felt I *should* do it. (The part, perhaps, that was being hidden—and *protected*—by my outward *cruelty*...) I went back— still scowling at this *responsibility* I felt—and found her crying (as I knew she would be). She was talking to a friend, and he politely excused himself. I walked up to her, and, in the face of her steady tears—which I knew that I (and I *alone*) had caused—my cruelty and anger suddenly melted. I apologized. I hugged her. Instead of feeling like I wanted to lash out and hurt everything in the world, I felt bad for what she was feeling, and (to be honest) for what *I* was feeling, too. When her tears stopped, I suggested we go where I had originally been heading, where—even through my rage—I knew that I needed to go...

(How do I end this, except by saying that, one day, I hope you can realize what I have recently come to realize...)

In the past, all my foul moods and melancholic fits were things I went through alone. In high school, I simply suffered—*alone*—maybe writing long, rambling essays, driven by my rage. My last days in Paris, I simply walked around the beautiful, nighttime streets—*alone*—in search of some sort of clarity or calm. Even with my first love—who had *told* me to call her, if I ever fell into a particularly bad mood—I simply kept it to myself. (That was also the sign our *love* was at its end...) So, when I found myself sitting on a bench—in front of the Quidditch field—*crying*, and telling her everything I was *feeling*, it was entirely new and out-of-character, for me...

(While everyone thanks me for what I have given to the team over the course of my four years, the reality is that I am so much more in debt than everyone else for what Quidditch has taken from me...)

She just sat there—*listening*—and occasionally saying something comforting, or asking a question to gently lead me onward. It wasn't what she *said* that mattered (as it almost never is), but rather the *way* she said it, with the patience and sympathy of someone who really knows how to sit quietly and *listen*. She was always a great listener, that way. (Me? I was always a terrible listener to her, trying to give her *wisdom*, or *life-lessons*, or *advice*—*Maybe you should think about what your mother is feeling*—when she was upset, and just wanted someone to *console* her...)

(For it is finally what you give of yourself and what you give away—energy, time, love—that makes you more joyous...)

"*Quidditch is my baby...*" was the key sentence of everything I told her that night, of everything I had felt during that day. How I had given so much of myself to Quidditch, over the years, and had helped to *form* it—perhaps more than any other person—into what it *was*. How it had been one of the *only* things in my life—and, so often, the *best* thing—for four years. How it had brought me *love*, and *friends*, and a *place* in the world. How it had made me *grow*, and *challenged* me, and *taught* me, and kept me in *shape*, and brought forth so many *insights*, and inspired so much of my *writing*, and finally got me to open *up* to the world, admitting that maybe—just maybe—I *liked* people and wanted to be *close* to them. But I would soon be leaving it, this thing that I loved so much. I would soon be leaving it behind—this thing that I had helped to *create*, and which had given me so much *happiness* throughout the years. I was like a parent, leaving his child behind, and having to watch it go out into the world—on its *own*—because you can no longer be there for it. I *loved* it—and wanted the *best* for it—but I also couldn't envision my life *without* it. (A parent's love is still so *selfish*, even as if it's the most *selfless* love there is...) If I didn't have it in my life to *love*, to take *care* of—to *cry* over—what would I have? *How could I let go of something that meant so, so much to me?*

(And for that you are infinitely grateful for all that your fellow Quidkids have been so wonderful to take from you...)

I wasn't just talking about Quidditch, though. That was what my mouth was saying—and what she was hearing—but that's not what my words really meant. I was also talking about my entire college *experience*, which I would be leaving in a month. This place where I had found a *home*, had fallen in *love*, had *changed* so much. This place where I had had so many *great* and *terrible* moments, the *terrible* moments only serving to make me ready and more willing to seek out *other*—and *better*—moments. I couldn't get my head around the thought of not being there—at college—*anymore*. Of never being able to return to that life—as I had lived it—for the past four years. Of no longer being a *student*, no longer taking the *classes* that I loved, no longer seeing everyone I *knew*, no longer going to *concerts* or *plays*, no longer playing *Quidditch*, no longer passing my life in this *place* that I loved so much. *How could I let go of something that meant so, so much to me?*

But I wasn't just talking about Quidditch, and I wasn't just talking about college. At the heart of my words—hidden by everything I was saying—I was talking about *her*: this person who sat next to me on the bench, listening to my confessions of how scared and *pained* all of this made me. I was talking to her—telling her my *deepest*, rawest feelings—but she didn't know (neither of us knew) that those feelings had more to do with *her,* than they did anything else. I wasn't strong enough to see—to admit to myself—that it was our *love* I was talking about, and which I was so terrified of losing. Our *love*, which was so *young* and so at all *beginning*, and which (so soon) was going to *leave* us—in a month, for all we knew. For we hadn't talked about what would happen—with *us*—at the end of the year. I was too scared to bring it up, too scared to even think about the thought of losing *her*—and losing this *love*—which had encircled and deeply guided my life for the past five months. *She meant so, so much to me—more than I could even say: how could I simply let her go?*

Only later would I realize what I had really been talking about that night, and what she had done for me. It was *her*—it was *her*, so many times— that broke me out of my terrible, dark, *self-enclosed* moods. That summer, it was the thought of her *dying*—coupled with a mutually loved song—which finally broke through to me, after a series of hurtful, crazed, and *mean* emails which I had sent to her, throughout the day. The next Fall—the last weeks we were together, before saying goodbye—she was there (again) when I broke down into tears. We had stayed together throughout the Summer, but—at the end of September (when I would be leaving for France)—that was the end for *us*, too. We had still had two more weekends together, though—weekends when I came back to this *place* that I had left, only a few months earlier: the *college* campus, the *Quidditch* field, so many scenes and settings of our *love*. I broke down, again—talking *around* things, as I had done before (talking about *childhood*, and the pain I still felt from it)—instead getting to the *heart* of what I was really feeling. She listened to me, though, and—like always—she was wonderful. Later, though, when she broke down (there were lots of tears those two weekends), all I could do was hold her, as *tightly*—and yet as *gently*—as I could. Because—unlike all those other times—I didn't have anything to say. There was nothing for me to say, this time—no nuggets of *wisdom* to share, no *advice* to give her—because I myself didn't know how to deal with what she (what *we*) were feeling. I couldn't even comfort her—*wordlessly*—as she had done for me, so many times. She was crying over our *end*—and over our *love*—as I had been crying over our *end* and our *love*, five months earlier. I didn't know how to make her feel better—I didn't know what to *say*, what to *do*—because the simple, terrible, unbearable fact was that our love was *ending*, and neither of us (no matter how much I *thought* I did) felt that was for the best...

23 Años de soledad

A friend once told me that I reminded her of Colonel Aureliano Buendía, one of the characters in Gabriel García Márquez's great, sprawling novel, *100 Years of Solitude*.

At the time, I took it as a *compliment*—Aureliano's a fascinating character, perhaps the most fascinating one in a book overflowing with the variety and *vitality* of human life. (*You're amazing...*) The novel opens inside his thoughts—the moment he is standing before a firing squad—having been captured after waging a seemingly noble, ten-years long *war* against the government of his country. But he doesn't think about any of that, standing before the firing squad, at the moment of his death—he thinks back to that moment (when he was five or six) when he saw *ice* for the first time...

What did my friend mean by that comparison? Aureliano was born with preternaturally open eyes, and it seemed to others like he was looking *through* them. (My gaze can seem *piercing* to those who catch it...) When he was young—and, more rarely, when he was older—he was able to *foresee* things, before they happened. (Things that I've said—or written— have later appeared *prophetic*...) He was rather old when he finally *lay with a woman*—perhaps because he was still haunted by that specter over whom he and his brother had once pined. (In me, there's this strange mix of outward *coldness* and fiery *passion* underneath...) Later—long after he finally slept with that woman—he meets a young girl, and thinks about her *constantly*, until he finally receives consent to marry her. (Other people have compared me to a *greyhound*, for the singular, obsessive *focus* that can absorb me...) Then, after his wife dies, he proceeds to start a revolution, favoring the side of the Liberals, off and on, for many years—not for any ideals or causes, as Aureliano admits in a memorable scene, but solely out of the strength and command of his *pride*. (It's not that hard to imagine me undertaking—for years and years—a perpetual, ultimately pointless war, all for the sake of *pride*...) To be honest, that is probably what most connects the two of us, and seems to make one a reflection of the other—the indefatigable, unquenchable, and unrepentant *pride,* of both Aureliano Buendía and myself.

Later on (when I read the novel a second time), I saw that *pride* in a different light. It wasn't necessarily something to be emulated or *admired*, but rather the force that gave to Aureliano the singular form of *solitude* in his life. Throughout the course of his life, Aureliano might burn with a sort of *flame*, but it's the *cold* flame of pride—like the coldness of *ice*. (*That day, when he was five or six*—he, unlike his brother, was drawn to the ice; he touched it, feeling something he had ever felt before, in his life...) In Aureliano, it's not the warm flame of *love*, like burns up the lives of so many other characters in the novel. Aureliano Buendía—this *fascinating* figure—can't *love*, at all...

§

Books change whenever we read them, whether because *we* change, or because we find something *new* in rereading them. Three years later—when I read *100 Years of Solitude*, again—I found myself drawn so much more to Amaranta, Aureliano's sister.

In her youth, Amaranta and her sister Rebecca both fall in love with the same man from Italy— Pietro Crespi—who has come to set up their pianola. When he chooses her sister, she experiences an insane *jealousy*, and spitefully—explicitly—tells Rebecca that she will *kill* her before ever letting the wedding go through. When the wedding is suddenly called off (the adopted Rebecca marries instead her not blood-related brother), Pietro soon falls in love with Amaranta herself, only for her to flatly— *eternally*—reject him. He kills himself. Amaranta intentionally burns herself on the stove, and—for the rest of her life—she wears a black veil over her hand, both to hide the scars and as a sort of *penance*. She soon fades into the background, as the rest of the stories play out in the novel. In her old age, she receives another marriage proposal—from Colonel Gerineldo Márquez, a retired general, and a friend of Aureliano. Every day, they sit together on the porch, she knitting, he smoking—no one doubts that she'll accept. But—once again—she flatly turns him down, shaking her head at the foolishness of such an idea. As children come and go throughout the house, Amaranta acts as a sort of *mother* to them. At some point, Aureliano José (one of the children she has raised) falls in love with her, and they have a brief but tempestuous affair. At the end—after she prophesizes her own death—she begins to receive messages from people all over the city, which she promises to take with her. She dies an old woman (having been correct in her fatal prophecy), and is covered with the funeral shroud which she— herself—has woven for just that occasion.

I never thought much about Amaranta, the first time I read the novel. That's the point, though—the life she lives seems far less interesting and *full* than that of her brother. As if—though she is always *present*—she always remains slightly out of the spotlight. Even in the major events of her life, she shares the stage with others—Rebecca, Aureliano José—and never seems herself to be the principal character of a scene. Everyone thinks of her—even her mother—as having been overcome by her own, wounded *pride*, which prevented her from finding anything *more* in her life, beyond the house in which she had always lived. That image, though, is completely altered about three-quarters of the way into the novel, when Ursula—her mother—comes to realize just what it was that drove Amaranta's fate: not *pride*—as everyone had believed—but *cowardice*, which prevented the deeply loving soul of her daughter from ever reaching *beyond* itself, out towards *another*...

Blind and essentially relegated to living in her memories, Ursula begins to see in the way that—perhaps—only the old and *infirm* can, discovering those truths of her family which have long remained hidden from view. One part of her discovery is the true cause of Amaranta's solitude; the other is her realization that Aureliano—her youngest son, and the one she has always seemed to loved most—is actually the person who has been overcome by "*pure and sinful pride*." And not only that (she realizes), but Aureliano—himself—is simply "*a man totally incapable of love...*" (*The firing squad—that fateful day—fails to carry out its orders, instead joining Aureliano as he continues his fight...Many women come to him—it's a tradition to send virgins to the soldiers, the night before a battle—and many children are begotten by him...Eventually, the government agrees to a settlement to end the war, the revolutionaries having seemingly achieved what they had been seeking for, the whole time...Only Aureliano realizes the truth: that—after so many years, and so much fighting—nothing has been achieved, and nothing ever will be achieved...He tries to take his own life, only being thwarted by the clever thinking of a doctor...*) The whole of Aureliano's life, Ursula realizes—all the *woman*, all the *children*, all the *wars*; all the *foresight*, *spite*, *coldness*, and *pride*—has been entirely without *love*, nothing more than the result of various consuming obsessions, all of which soon faded away...

Every character in the novel has their own form of *solitude*—for some it's their *dreams*; for others it's their *lust*, or their *past*. If Aureliano's solitude comes from his *pride*—his inability to *love*—what does that say about me? (It takes great *pride* to try to write a book—but also great *love*...) But if—upon rereading—I see myself more and more in Amaranta and her *cowardice*, what does *that* say? (It would be *cowardly* to write about your *desire* for love, instead of actually seeking *out* that love, in your own, real *life*...) Which of these varied and terrible *solitudes* am I condemned to, each of them like another circle of *Hell* in Dante's *Inferno*?

(*And how does the story end?*) After the war, Aureliano returns—so many years later—to his childhood home, and proceeds to burn each and every trace of his existence[6]. (*For to see myself thus*

6 Except for a single photograph—of his deceased wife—which his mother manages to save...

reflected in the black shroud of Amaranta's perpetual virginity...) He spends the rest of his days holed up in his workshop, making little fishes out of gold. *(To see her so willing and so capable of inspiring love, but for all that unable to navigate the waters so as to actually experience that love...)* For a time he sold the fishes, until he learned that people were collecting them as relics of the war hero *Colonel Aureliano Buendía*. *(A childless mother, a virgin not out of coldness but out of the uncontained purity of her passion...)* Then, he simply began melting the ones he had made, in order to make them all over again. *(Who doesn't trust herself and/or life to hazard the unknown alleyways of openness and love...)* He dies on a foggy day, watching a military parade pass by—an old, wasted man, wrapped in a filthy blanket, and still flickering with the pride that has burned throughout his whole life. *(But one who, for all that, never lets anything go...)*

01.11.11, 02.21.13

Before leaving for Paris (two years ago), I never once imagined what the experience would be like. I never once thought about where I would *go*—or what I would *do*—when I was there. I never thought—in *details*, with concrete *images*—what it would be like to live in a foreign country, or to speak another language, or to start a new life, somewhere else. (Never imagined myself walking along the *Seine*, or visiting the *Eiffel Tower*, or drinking a glass of wine in a quintessentially *French* restaurant...)

Later (once I had been in Paris a few months) I mentioned to my host mother that I hadn't imagined my stay—hadn't formed any *expectations* for it—before arriving. It was this (I told her), which had kept me firmly grounded in the *present*, able to fully immerse myself in all the new, different, and *taxing* experiences that I had had, during my stay. It had also been due to this consummate *presence* (along with my singular *determination*) that I had been able to gain—in only three months time—a rather strong command of my new language. (*You speak French...*) Before I had arrived in Paris, I had only taken two and half years of French, and—admittedly—I lacked both the prolonged exposure and the inherent confidence to *thrive* in the language, at first. A tremendous effort, though, along with a single-minded *obsession*—one which remains firmly entrenched in the *present*, focusing all its attention on the task in front of it—can (slowly, gradually) achieve even the greatest and most *far-off* goals...

Or, at least, that was what I believed. That was what I *told* myself, rather. It's true that I was focused entirely on what was in front of me, during those three months, but I was not *present*. I was not *happy*, I was not really *open*, I did not love *my* life or *life*, itself. My dedication to learning French had acted as its own sort of *escape* from the present, and from all the reality that I didn't want to deal with or *face*. I was running *away* from so much—the past, primarily—but I was also terrified and lost, because I also didn't know where I was running *to*. (Of course, we can't know what we're running *towards*— not until we turn around, and finally stop staring at what we've been running *from*...)

I hadn't imagined the future—hadn't planted in the ground any dreams or expectations—because I had been too *scared* to do so. It was like there was a *wall* in my life—firmly built upon January 10—past which neither my imagination, nor my thoughts, nor my *hopes* could go. To look beyond that date would have been to acknowledge what—all too soon—I would be *confronting*: this completely *unforeseeable*, largely *uncontrollable*, and entirely new and *foreign* experience, which I didn't know if I could handle. If I had simply looked at myself, I would have seen how *excessive* my attitude had been, before leaving. Either I finished all my preparations—all those endless papers, documents, supplies that I would need— *immediately*, as soon as I received them; or I took *forever* to get things done, procrastinating until the very last minute. Both of these attitudes were excessive—they *meant* too much, they required too much *energy*. They were the disproportionate reactions of one who either *fights*—or *flies*—without any sort of balance or moderation in-between. I didn't even like talking about my trip, because I didn't want to *think* about it. Or: I was *constantly* thinking (and worrying) about it, but I didn't want to talk to people, didn't want to see just how *real* my trip was, and how—all too soon—it was really going to *happen*. That's what *Paris* was, for me: a looming, unfocused and terrifying *idea*, one which I didn't see in terms of images or details, but which I felt *deeply* in my body, and which my thoughts blankly—*terrifyingly*—revolved around...

It might be expected that—after spending so much time in *self-reflection*—I would finally *learn* some things about myself. And it's true—I have learned some things—but that knowledge doesn't always stop me from committing (once again) the same, *scared* actions as I did, in the past. (Knowledge may allow us to see ourselves *clearer*,

but it does not make what we see any *better*...)
For, in going (once again) to France—two years
later—I acted in the same, *scared* way as before.
Either I put off everything until the very, very
end—knowing, the whole time, all the tasks that I
should be doing—or I had to will myself into crazy,
frenzied *fits*, just to get things done. I had to sit
down and *force* myself to work—for an hour or
two—before ripping myself away, exhausted and
unable to handle any more thought of the *future*.
This time, at least—two years later—I knew what
I was doing. I knew that my refusal to confront the
future came from that *horror* I felt, staring into the
impenetrable darkness of *Possibility* and *Life* that
awaited me, on the other side...

I had not truly been *present*, either before Paris, or
during my first few months there. (I was not *present*,
either, before coming back to France, or during my
first few months here...) That was just the ingenious,
backward-looking *interpretation* through which I tried
to build a more flattering and self-inflating history
than had actually been the case. By the end, I *was*
open and alive to the full experience of Paris, but
that didn't mean I had been open at the *beginning*.
My refusal to think of the future had been born from
fear, even if—in the end—it had led to something
great, *alive*, *open*, and *honest*. Not honest enough—
however—to admit the dark and *fear-governed* place

from which it had initially sprung. No matter how honest I may have been—with myself—about who I *was*, at that moment, I still was not honest enough (with myself) to admit who I had been, *before*. I invented these beautiful, believable stories about being *present* in order to efface the presence of *fear* in my past, and in order to forget (let's be honest) just how *easily* that fear could come back into my life—or, perhaps, was already *there*—even if I seemed to be so *happy*, in the present…

Those first months in Paris, I had been living in the dreamlike non-existence of *obsession*. I was paying so much attention to *one* thing—learning the French language—in order to ignore everything *else*. In order to *escape* from everything else, which I couldn't really bear to pay attention to, or to *feel*. I was living in the *past*, I was living in *dreams*—I was living anywhere you like—but I was not living in the *present*. The future may not be *real*, but our hopes for the future—our desires to reach after more experience—*are* real. When I couldn't hope for the future, couldn't form expectations, couldn't dream, couldn't imagine, that was because I couldn't stand to reach after life—to reach after *more* life—in the form of anything *alive, deep, risky, dangerous, unlimited,* or *real.* (*I had never—not once—imagined a* real *future with her…*)

§

The last weekend that I visited her, I had conceived of one, final *grand romantic gesture*—an *inversion* of that date which I had planned, four months earlier. Instead of going back over all the *past* we had lived together, we would go on a journey—in the imagination—through all those possible *futures* that we could have together, past September 23, 2012:

1) staying together, working hard at it, until December when I begin pulling away and it ends bitter and yelling over Skype...

2) asking her to leave behind school and run away to France with me...

3) she literally trapping me in her dorm room and not letting me leave...

4) staying together, weathering the distance, then seeing each other the following summer, still keeping it alive...

5) stay together, until about a month in, when we mutually decide that we can't take it and agree— through great sadness—to end it...

6) she finds someone else...

7) I find someone else...

Then—at the end of these reveries—I would look at her and say: *All these visions—beautiful, ridiculous, realistic, painful, impossible—are only that, visions,* *because the reality is that, right now, it's ending, and we're not staying together...*Rightly or wrongly—smartly or foolishly—I didn't actually do this date, only told her about her. She understood, too, just how *bittersweet* it would have been: how much nothing in the world could have been *sweeter* than the date, as long as we were on it—sailing on a raft through our own imagined futures—but how *bitter* it would have been when it finally ended, and we saw just how *crushing* the reality really was. Because, for me, this date and its visions were never anything more than that, *imaginings*, and never—not for one *moment*—did I ever see any *hope* in them, for reality. Or, at least, that's what I *told* myself—because (looking back on it, now) how could I imagine without *hope*? How can you imagine a *future*, without the indefiniteness of an *always*—an implicit *forever*—right there, at the center, giving *life* to that imagination and making it *possible*? (*I was too scared to love her* forever...)

§

So many people talk of love as being *forever*, and there's something deeply *true* to that. I don't think love is or can be *forever*, in reality—time passes, love fades, people die—but I think the crux of love is that it *wants* to be forever. Love *aspires* to *forever*, *dreams* of *forever*, *hopes* with all its soul for *forever*, foolishly and impossibly tries to achieve that *forever* in *reality*. That's what love *is*—knowing no bounds; or, knowing them, but still striving *against* them, nonetheless. Love is not full, if it's held back and restrained—checked and inhibited— by *time*, or *expiration dates*, or *fear*, or *death*. We don't love fully, if we hold ourselves back from those unlimited dreams and desires—for the future, for *forever*—which are the natural consequences of love's overflowing of the *present*. We don't love as much as we could have, if we don't let our hopes and dreams—and our *love*—run free, spreading outward and blanketing the sky in beautiful *possibilities*, and even more beautiful *impossibilities*. After all, wasn't it only after we had a future—a future spread into the endlessness of *Summer*—that we finally admitted what we *meant* to each other, and I (that same, fateful night) found myself saying those three, simple words? (*The first avowal…*)

§

I often think back to a story—*Extreme Solitude*, by Jeffrey Eugenides—which I read many years ago. I didn't like the story that much, the first time I read it; in fact, I was rather *critical* of it. (*Once the first avowal has been made…*) And yet I found myself coming back to this story—again and again— throughout the years, especially to the ending, when Madeleine (the protagonist) is suddenly overcome (mid-coitus, crying, and looking into her lover's face) with *feeling*, and can no longer hold herself back from saying it. (*Once the first avowal has been made, "I love you"...*) He—her lover—doesn't say anything, though. He gets up, takes up a book out of her bag, and hands it to her to read. (And why didn't I like the story?) The book he hands her is Barthes' magnificently painful work, *A Lover's Discourse*—in particular, the section on "*I Love You*". (Because I thought it misunderstood the way(s) that *post-modernism* feels about *love*...) Madeleine reads the book—dutifully—until she gets to the line: "*Once the first avowal has been made, "I love you" has no meaning whatever...*" Then, she looks up at him—at this person she *loves*—and throws the book at his head...

And if she had known what I was thinking, that first time I said it—when the only thing my words were expressing was the desire to save her pain or *embarrassment* (and to save *me* the hassle and consequences)—would she, in real life, have acted any differently? For when she had *hinted* at it, that night—a hint which I couldn't help but *hear*—I knew how *hard* it would be for her to say it, the first time. I knew that *I* should say it—that she wanted it to be *me* who said it—that first time. And so I said it. I said it, thinking (to myself) that I was just chronologically *altering* the truth—trying to write a happier, more *loving* story—because I knew that one day I would both *say* it and *mean* it. (And I did! Later, I did!) But, in that moment—not quite being ready, my hand being forced—I knew that saying it, then, would save us (*both* of us) so much embarrassment and so much *pain*, without her being any the wiser about the deeply *fictional* nature of it all. (*I had never loved her as much as I* could *have...*)

§

I had always thought that my love, whatever else it had been—*short*, *tumultuous*, *fucked up*, *scared*—was, at least when it was *good*, the sort of total and utter *love* that we rarely allow ourselves in life. I always thought that, at least, I had loved her—deeply, as much as I could have—when I *did* love her, even as I was *mean* to her, or said stupid things, or pulled away constantly and in ever new (but fundamentally the *same*) ways. But even in the Spring—even in our best and *highest* moments, at the end of April and the beginning of May—even then I didn't have such a full and *honest* love. And, later— as soon as the end-date of September 23rd began to loom—my love, too, started to pull away, to close up into itself. (Like a river, which can no longer flow *unhindered...*) Yes, it might have been because I was leaving for France for seven months (at least), and I knew that staying together wouldn't be a good idea. That doesn't change the fact, though, that my love was still *bounded*—always circumscribed to a set *date*—and never felt that limitless rushing towards *forever* which love indulges in, that endless reaching towards the *future* through which love grows and subsists. For those four months—all through the Summer, and leading up to the end—my love was tentative and half-hearted, at best. (*I had never loved her* fully...)

§

During the semester before I left (the first time) for France, I took a class on meditation—something I had never done before. At that time, I was just starting (once again) to inhabit the *present*—small, weak, frail, and *convalescent*, as I was. And that— above all—what was I learned from meditating: how to remain *present*, and truly aware of the *moment*, not letting my thoughts fly off into the *future*—into *dreams*, or impossible, soaring *hopes*—but learning to live with my own, present *emptiness*. Of course (soon enough), I stopped meditating. *Paris* was looming, and my fears of the *future*—along with my need to run away from the *past*—meant that I largely left behind whatever sort of true *presence* I had attained during that semester. (But that's also the time when we *most* need something—precisely when it's farthest from us, and we are *least* inclined to seek it out...)

My entire time in France—this time around—I could only get myself to meditate once, sometime near the end of Winter. It was only for 15 minutes, though, because I was out of practice. (I hadn't meditated in over two years, despite thinking—frequently—that I *should* be doing it...) And when I opened my eyes, at the end of those 15 minutes—15 minutes of simply trying to be as *present* as possible—a succession of thoughts suddenly rushed in upon me, one which (perhaps) could only come to me then, in my *emptiness*:

I had never loved her fully...I had never loved her as much as I could have...I was too scared to love her forever...I had never—not once—imagined a real future with her...

§

Later, on the cusp of leaving—once again—for France, I felt myself (once again) *powerless* in the face of the future. And, at the end of Summer—one of the last weekends we would spend together—my *love* for her, too, dwindled, diminished, *shrank*. And I cried. Because all I could think about was the *future*—of a time when I would be gone, and she would (eventually) be with someone else. Visions kept on coming before my eyes (waking nightmares that I couldn't stop) of her and someone *else*—someone who was a real individual, existing in the world, but who really only stood for the *Future*: that *Future*—full of new *experiences*, new *places*, new *thoughts*, and new *feelings*—which I would never have with her. All those *hopes* and *fears* of hers that I would never know, all those *smiles* and *tears* that would come and disappear without ever touching me in the slightest, no matter how much (and how accurately!) I may have been able to imagine them, from afar. She would go off, and live her own life, and—even if she didn't find someone *else*, even if she didn't stop caring about *me*—one day *Life* would come and take her away, lifting her off her feet and taking her to places that I never would (never *could*) go. *One day you'll forget all about me*...And she would *have* to forget about me (wouldn't she?), because that's what it means to *live*, and to *continue* to live. (And—also—to *move on*?) I knew that—I *knew* it—but I still couldn't keep that most terrible of thoughts (of being *forgotten*) from breaking my heart. I couldn't take it—couldn't do anything to *stop* it—as all these horrible, jealous visions came passing before my eyes. All I could do was watch (mutely, and in horror) as the *Future*—as *Life*—was coming to take her away from me...

§

I *had* wanted a future with her—I just had never let myself *see* it. I had held myself back from the *fullness* of love (*I had never loved her* fully...), held myself back from giving *everything* (*I had never loved her as much as I could have...*), held myself back from daring to hope that our love would last as far as the eye could see—or the mind could travel—off into that endless horizon of *forever* (*I was too scared to love her* forever...) *I had never—not once—imagined a real future with her...* Not until the end, that is. (Not until it was *over...*) Then— suddenly—I found myself rushing into the *future*, my eyes filling with all these visions of what *could* be between us (*Long-distance...Through her years in college...After she graduated...*) Visions—things which I had never let myself *imagine*, before—of what it all could have *been* (*Getting married...Having children... Dying...*) *Could* have been, because—*now*—it was over. And only now that it was *over*, could I finally indulge all those feelings—all those *hopes*—which I had kept myself (so long) from admitting. But hope springs forth—whether we like it or not, whether we *want* it to or not—*eternally*. When I held myself back from dreaming of the *future*, I held myself back from *hoping*, held myself back from loving her as *fully*—and as *forever*—as I *could* have. (*But why?*)

Honestly, I have been asking—over and over and over again—my entire life: *How can you love something, without* wanting *to have it—and wanting to have it,* forever? (Or, in other words: *How can you love something that is going to* die?) So I hold myself back, I restrict my dreams—suppress them, pretend that I never have them, act like that I don't really have any *hope* in their becoming *real*. (*And why do I do that?*) Because I once had let my *hope* run away into beliefs of *forever*, and I had been burned, burned so badly that I never wanted to get close to such hopes—such *life*— again...

01.20.97, 08.15.07

When I was seven, my first pet—a goldfish named Pigfish—died. (I had taken his name from another fish, which my oldest sister had once had....) A day or two before, I had one of those fatal *premonitions*—inspired by someone's illness—when you both *fear* (and secretly *know*) that the end might be coming. But I was seven, and the only forms that this prophetic feeling took were an over-sensitivity to things and a hyper-vigilant *attention* to the health of my fish.

We had just returned from visiting my grandmother—my father's mother, who had recently suffered a major, debilitating stroke—when I found him. (I sometimes find myself saying that we had been returning from my Nana's *funeral*—events which, in reality, happened three years apart...) I ran to the fishbowl as soon as I was through the front door, *fearing* (and secretly *expecting*) the worst.

I don't remember what happened after that—not until the moment when I was in my bedroom, with my tear-stained eyes fixed (immovably) on the cloth rainbow hanging on my wall. My mother was there, holding me and trying to make me feel better—but it didn't help. I remember how nothing could help, and I just cried and cried, staring at this rainbow but feeling like there was something so dark and *colorless* around me. (*Perhaps I had fed him too much, had loved him too well!*)

(Time passed...) In seventh grade, I wrote an essay—elegiac and *cliché*—on Pigfish. (Tragic *cliché* by a thirteen-year old, though, should *always* be forgiven...) That was my year of *elegies*—I also wrote one about my grandmother's death. The main goal of that paper was to convey the particular sort of hazy, purple *unreality* that I found myself moving in, after she died. (*"I felt as if the world was no more"*, *"But she couldn't be dead, she just couldn't"*—things like that...) The pivotal moment in the *haze* (though I didn't write about this) came when I was talking to my Mom about a party—the first boy/girl party in our class—which I had been invited to. Everyone had been *asking* me, and *asking* me—because I hadn't decided, couldn't make up my mind. I don't know why, really—there was no reason *not* to go, that I could formulate. It was—seemingly—just pure *indecision*, a complete inability to *act*. (As would become a *theme*, throughout my life...) Everything boiled over when my Mom, too, asked me about the party, and—exasperated, helplessly *angry*—I said something about having to ask *"my stupid Mom"* first. (That didn't go over well, obviously...) I didn't mean it, but I also couldn't take the words back, once I had said them. (There are certain things you can never take back, no matter how much you may *want* to...)

(Back to the story...) Most of the time, Pigfish was—for me—nothing more than a passing remark that my mother or I would make to each other, when we saw that the flowers grew well in certain spots of our garden. (We had frozen his body, and then planted it as fertilizer, in the Spring...) It wasn't until I was going to therapy—twelve years after these memories were formed—that Pigfish came *forcefully* back into my life. I was not a proponent of therapy, but even I had to admit the value of being compelled to revisit memories—out loud, and *emotionally*—that you normally wouldn't want to face. One day, Pigfish came up, and I found myself reliving that moment—sitting on my bed—when I was crying, but my mother couldn't do anything to help me. I was *alone* in my pain, and no one—not even my own *mother*—could take it away or lessen it. Tears came to my eyes (twelve years later), as I was struck by the realization that I had *always* been alone. It was something I knew (all too well) that day when I was six, and it had always been true, all that time—all those twelve *years*—in-between. I had *always* been alone, because no one could really *affect* me—really *touch* me—either in *pain*, or in *joy*. No one could access the *feelings* that I had, no one could *change* them or take them *away*, no one could reach across the borders of my own *skin* so as to make me feel—even for a second—like I wasn't *alone*, and always *had* been. In that moment, the entire color of my life—from birth to present—altered, suddenly becoming so much *darker* than it had been, only a few moments before. Or, at least, I now saw—with my own eyes—all that empty *space*, separating each and every *body*, from every *other* one...

§

(Skip back some time—hours, days, *years*...) My class was in the library—either working (without much haste) on some sort of project, or simply having free time to read and find books. Somehow, between myself and one of the girls in my class, the idea of an imaginary *fish*—an imaginary fish, which was *mine*—came up. Maybe I saw a fish in a book, and made a comment about how it was mine. Maybe I was just spurred into creating an imaginary *pet*, like I had been for a year or two. Whatever the source, it soon came to pass that other students were in on the game, treating this fish as *real*—and as *mine*—too. The next thing I know, the girl (the one with whom I had first begun the game) has her hands cupped together, palms up, and is telling me—with a look of play-acted *sadness*, on her face—that my fish is *dead*...

It's possible that I *provoked* her, with an unkind word, or something else to which a first-grader takes offense. It has never seemed important to me whether—in that first action—I was guilty or not, because it would soon be overshadowed by a guilt both larger and more *lasting*. She held out her hands, telling me my dead fish was in them. I slapped them. (*I slapped them...*) I don't remember (for how could I?), but in this memory I always think that my face must have become instantaneously *grotesque*, something so stricken by *horror* and *rage* as to become unrecognizable. I don't think she cried, either. I remember a look of cold *shock* on her face, as if she was hurt only by the *surprise* of the game ending—suddenly—and in this unfun way: emotionally *jolted*, rather than hurt, *physically*. I went back to my table, and cowered into myself—not interacting with anyone or anything—wanting to *disappear...*

Later that day—once we had returned to our classroom—I sat down and waited, *fearing* (and *expecting*) the worst. Finally, the moment came, and the teacher called me to her desk. She recited what she had been told. I don't know if I said anything, if I tried to deny what the witness had said, if I tried to argue for my own side, if I tried to do anything—anything, at *all*—except to *survive*, this moment. She told me to *flip my star* (the punishment system in our classroom), and to put it at *one* (the lowest level of infraction). But you probably don't understand how much that *meant* to my first-grade self, who had not flipped his star (*not once!*) the entire year, at least six months in. (*You're perfect...*) In that moment, it felt like the *end of the world*—not to have been *caught*, not to be in *trouble*, but to have lost my hold on pure and utter *perfection*, which I knew (once gone) I could never get back, again...

(Later, that summer—or maybe several summers later—I found my star from first grade, with its single blemish on the number *one*. In a fit of fevered *panic*, I poked holes in the other four numbers, as well, telling myself that—this way—I would no longer be able to find any *trace* of my misconduct, and—this way—I would soon be able to *forget* my failure...Of course, the only thing that rash act did was to solidify my memory even more, and to ensure that—now—I can *never* forget what happened...)

The world took on a strange appearance, walking from the wall of stars back to my seat. People asked me what happened, but I just shrugged them off, not saying anything. I just felt *empty*, completely cut off from *everything*—and *everyone*—in the world. There was this unreal *clarity* to everything I saw—as if the outline of every object was so much *sharper* than it had been before, almost *living*. The world had *changed*, for me, and, in this new world—filled with this unreal *clarity*—I saw just how *distant* I now was (separated by an uncrossable *void*) from any sort of *perfection* that could ever be achieved, in life.

The funny thing is that (later) my Mom recounted the story of how much my first grade teacher had *loved* me. In particular, how—at the end of the year—my teacher had flipped my star *herself*, not because I had done anything wrong, but because it wouldn't have been a good (a *smart?*) idea to let me retain a sense of my own *perfection*. I knew that it (this story my Mom was telling) wasn't *true*, but I didn't say anything—perhaps because I still wanted, so badly (a decade, and a high school graduation— as valedictorian!—later), for that *happier* version to be true. But these memories—from first grade— are the earliest and most *vivid* that I have, and I couldn't (*can't*) forget them, even if I tried...

§

I sat, without speaking—in a chair across from my therapist—as all these thoughts rolled over me. He tried to get me to talk—to tell him what I was thinking and feeling—but I couldn't. I was literally *choked up*—something which I had always just thought was an *expression*. The whole story of my life was *changing*, before my eyes—and I was watching it with mute and horrific *fascination*—when he looked at the clock, and told me it was time to go. I looked at him, saw *sadness* in his eyes (perhaps *pity* for my feelings, or *pity* for kicking me out), but I still couldn't believe that he was telling to go, now—*now*—when I was most in need of *help*. (All those other times that I didn't want to be there, didn't want to go to therapy—didn't want help from him, or from *anyone*—but in this moment, *here*, *now*, when I actually needed to be helped—to be *touched*, to be *assuaged*, to be *prodded*—this was the one time he was telling me to leave!) I couldn't believe it. My wordlessness turned from sorrow into *anger*, as if the *emptiness* I now felt were not an absence but a sort of *overflowing*, so sensitive that it would break out—in *rage*—towards any object that produced the slightest provocation.

I didn't say anything, either, as my mother drove home. I looked out at the transfigured world, and felt within myself a transfigured understanding. Everything in the world seemed clarified by *pain*, as if every *body* were separated—by an invisible *eternity*—from every *other*. My whole life, too, seemed clarified by pain—I finally saw the true character of all those attempts at *love* and *connection* that had failed in my life, and which had always been *destined* to fail. There was no lingering and undaunted *hope*, no inspiration to *overcome* barriers—or to *strive*, nonetheless—after this realization. The only thing I got from it was a pervasive sense of that *loneliness* which I always had known in my life (since my pet—Pigfish—had died), and which I always *would* know, in my life. (And which was all my *fault*...)

03.20.06, 06.28.08

He probably wouldn't recognize me today. I look the same—with longer hair—and my soul (at its core) probably looks the same, but most everything between the two has changed: the way I *talk*, the way I *write*, the way I *live*. If we were to see each other today, what would we even have to say? (*And how should we begin?*)

§

(It [the artist's work] is always aimed at least partly over the heads of your fellow man...)

§

We knew each other in high school, when *passion* was still the highest value—the more foolish, the better. We weren't any sort of high school *hedonists* or *lotharios*, though. We were *artists*, who (at least as we saw them) are constantly seeking their own sorts of *excesses—life*, *death*, *creation*, and the most spiritualized, unrealizable *love* you could ever imagine. We didn't really have friends, outside of each other. (At least I didn't...) And we weren't really *friends*, either—more like the person you talk to as if you were talking to *yourself*. If we needed each other, it was only with the most unabashedly *self-centered* need. (At least for me...) If we ever got something from each other, it was the same as if we had been reading a good, insightful *book*. (Like that pivotal book, which first brought us together...) If we *cared* about each other, it was only because we would have been *lost* without having that book—one which had ears, and could talk back to you...

§

(The last time I saw him was that summer night, when he was leaving—for good—to start a new life in Texas...)
(The last I heard of him, his family was looking for him—not knowing where he was, or what state he was in—but trying to get him professional help, and fearing for the worst...)

§

We were assholes to everyone but each other— he, explicitly; me, (mostly) in thought—and we didn't even feel guilty about it. Or, at least, the way we talked—about the necessity of focusing only on *ourselves* and our own *greatness*—never seemed to suggest, otherwise. (I did feel remorse—deep down—but I *desperately* tried to ignore it...) The artist owed it to himself—we owed it to *ourselves*— to do whatever needed to be done: putting *creation* above everything else, detaching from everything (and everyone) in quest of the perfect *work*, dedicating yourself completely to the search for

Art and *Greatness*. For the Artist (as we argued) cannot abide by half-measures, but must be willing to give up *everything* and *anything*—to leave behind (at a moment's notice) father or mother, sister or brother, God, *Beauty*, or *friend*—should the need ever arise. That's the price of what the Artist must go through, and *nothing*—not even the remonstrances of our family, or those closest to us—should be able to hold *him* (hold *us*) back. The Artist (so we believed) is an entity unto himself— and must *remain* unto himself—saying *fuck it* to everyone and everything else, because that's what *Art* really is, and what *Greatness* really demands. (*Greatness* demands *selfishness*...)

§

(These are the only genuine ideas; the ideas of the shipwrecked. All the rest is rhetoric, posturing, farce. He who does not really feel himself lost, is without remission; that is to say, he never finds himself, never comes up against his own reality...)

§

We disagreed on everything, and nothing. Which is to say: we were constantly using words *different*—and even *contradictory*—to each others', in order to say what we both knew (both *trusted*) was the same. His father made him go to *therapy*— he thought he was more in the right than the *therapist.* And I agreed with him—both for *him*, and for *myself.* (*What did I know?*) I knew him, or at least I knew the part of myself which I *found* in him. He—as the Artist—didn't need *therapy*: what he needed was *understanding* and *love.* Half of our discussions revolved endlessly around whatever philosophical, aesthetic, psychological, or religious ideas currently enthralled us. The other half (if only implicitly) was that fundamental desire which we—both of us, in our own ways—always sought: to be *loved*, and to be *understood.* (But only through *Art*, because that promised us *perfect* understanding, and a *perfect* love...)

§

(And the price of this kind of almost "extra human" creativity is to live on the brink of madness, as men have long known...No wonder he appears to average men as "crazy": he is not in anything's world...)

§

He came to me—by the end—with all his hopes and his fears, his anxieties and his crises (which were not infrequent). By the end, I was totally honest with him, too—but my honesty had also ceased being as *unflinching* as it (once) had been. One of our last days together (at least the last *good* day), we simply spent an hour together—sitting in the same room—and hardly saying anything, at all. We didn't really *need* to say anything, either—besides a few words, here and there—to know what the other was thinking. We had had that much time— that much *honest* time—together, to be able to do so. (*You just get me…*) But there was also a distance between us, at the end. Maybe it was just that we were both beginning new lives—he was going off to Texas, to become an artist; and I was going off to college—and had agreed (for good) to leave each other behind. (We had decided—at most—to meet only once more in our lives: when we were *old*, and could both look back on how much we had *changed*, and how much we had stayed the *same…*) It was more than that, though—at least for *me*. I felt like I had *outgrown* him. Like I was ready for something *new*. Like I had gotten all that I could get out of our relationship, out of those shared *ideas* and mutual *honesty* that had carried us—for so long—on such parallel, *yearning* paths…

§

(We might even say that the psychotic uses blatantly, openly, and in an exaggerated way the same kinds of thought-defenses that most people use wishfully, hiddenly, and in a more controlled way, just as the melancholic uses blatantly the defenses of the milder, more "normal" depressions of the rest of us…)

§

I've learned enough to realize how much of a pattern that is in my life: to push people away from me—to convince myself that I'm *over* them, *done* with them—when they're leaving my life. To reject *them*—to keep them from rejecting *me*—in leaving. (Oh, how predictable—and predictably *pathetic*—I am!) I didn't think we were friends, for the longest time. I didn't need people—and he didn't need anyone, either—but we both *gained* and *profited* enough from our interaction that we cultivated it and (greatly) sought it *out*. We had our own little *world*, into which other people couldn't really enter. I remember one lunch we ate together, along with a mutual acquaintance—a shy, but excessively witty young man[7]—who we each took turns talking *to*. Or, rather, who we each took turns talking *at*—because we both knew that we were only talking to *each other*, through the means of this third person. (To make it a little more *interesting*, for both of us…) Originally—in Junior year—we had been in Philosophy Club together. By senior year, though, everyone else in the club had stopped coming, and our meetings became—literally—what (in essence) they had always *been*: just the two of us talking—one to the other—in a classroom, after school. We didn't really *want*—or *need*—anyone else there. (They probably sensed that, too…) Not even

---

7 The same young man who once explained my own philosophy—pithily, and perhaps not inaccurately—back to me: *"Everything is nothing…"*

our favorite teacher—whose classroom we used, and whose class had first *enflamed* our souls—could really enter into our discussions, which only *we* knew (instinctively) how to stop or start...

§

Mr. A—:
(One of the only—non-fictional—persons I have ever looked up to....)

Thank you for helping me to play the game so well with the college and scholarship search. Even if you might not like the result, the book you gave me changed my life, at least, like you said, by "accelerating" the process that much faster...

(A role model, to put it simply—but the kind who you soon grow *dissatisfied* with, and *disappointed* in...)

However, I disrespect you because you gave me Denial of Death. *I respected you a lot for giving it to me, but now you aren't aspiring towards greatness, you aren't living up to that expectation I have for you...*

(I couldn't understand how he could teach the things he taught—and open up my eyes, the way he had—and still only live like he was living, failing to go *far* enough...)

But if you're content, that's all that will ever matter. I enjoy talking to you, I will admit, because you think, and care, and that's all I ask of those I communicate with...

(As he said to me, at some point: "*M— was right— you are a philosophical black hole...*")

And I wouldn't mind talking to you again sometime, if you wish to converse with a fervent egoist and individualist. -Dan Bossert

("You consume everything around you, let's just hope you spit it out the right way...")

§

I always worried (felt *guilty*) about potentially ruining the lives of those relatively stable, *normal* people around me—those who probably wouldn't have entered into such a *painful* vision of life, if I had not led them there. I never regretted it with M——, though, because it was *his* choice. I didn't force anything on him—my *melancholy*, my *idealism*, or my *darkness*. If anything, he led *me* to many of these ideas. Only now do I see how little I had to fear about hurting everyone *else*—they could (and did) take it in stride, because they had enough support and a firm enough *grounding* in their lives, to do so. It was *him*—it was *always* him—that I was most hurting. Unlike the others, we had the most to *gain* by our words and our ideas—and also the most to *lose*. The two of us (we believed) were closer to *living* those ideas, than everyone else. But he didn't really have the ability to *handle* them, not like I did. Because—deep down—I always *knew* that I could handle it. I always knew (no matter how much I tried to ignore it) that I was more on the side of the *angels*—the safe, secure, and *stable* ones—than in that other world, which he knew all too well. I should've *known* that I was stronger than him, in that sense. *Stronger*—perhaps—precisely because I was so far from *living* all of those ideas we talked about, and he was so *close* to them...

§

(Did I know he was going this way?)
(And if I did, does that make what I did *better*—or *worse*—or the *same*?)

§

(The artist disguises the incongruity that is the pulse-beat of madness but he is aware of it...)

§

To be honest, I don't know if I've ever met someone definitively *smarter* than me. (He, too, admitted that I was smarter...) But I can also admit that he was more wholly, truly *dedicated* to one thing—to *Art*—than I, myself, have ever been. To me, he will always be the *Artist*. Because he (the Artist) did whatever needed to be done—and gave up whatever needed to be given up—in order to get the art *made*. Because even then, I could see that I wasn't—truly—an artist, not like he (a painter, primarily) was an *artist*. What I wanted—more than anything else in the world— was to *live*. He—the Artist—only wanted to make the perfect *work*. I wanted to *experience* everything, and to live only for *today*. He only wanted to live for *tomorrow*, sacrificing the present in order to *create*. I said that I wanted *love*; he only *hinted* at such desires, through the unguarded hopes and dreams he told me. To me, the most beautiful thing he ever created was not a painting, or a drawing, or even a poem, but the *image*—as he once described it to me—of the *daughter* he would (one day) have. (*They lived, just the two of them, in a brownstone in New York; and—on her seventh birthday—he took her to the Brooklyn Zoo, where they spent the day together...*) He would have been the most loving father, in the world...

§

(*Even more than that, as the parents had opposed the child's natural energetic and free expansion and had determined his surrender to their world, they could be considered in some fundamental ways as guilty for whatever warpings his character had...*)[8]

§

---

8 What is being argued against, at least in part.

Let's be clear: he was 6ft6 or 7, red-headed, with pale skin, freckles, and long gangly limbs. He was perpetually slouching, even when he walked. He had a fiery glimmer in his eyes, surrounded by the most unexpressive face. He was usually hunched over a paper—drawing—even during class, only occasionally lifting his head to either look quizzically around the room, or to say something equally well-thought out and *bizarre*. He had been in and out of therapy—in and out of institutions—severely estranged from his family, who still tolerated him living in their house. His mother died when he was five, and no one ever explained to him what happened. His most poignant memory (for me) was when he was hiding under a table—at her funeral—scared and not knowing what was going on. I first knew him as the hilariously eccentric kid who listened to lots of rap music and tried to break-dance. Later, my mother mentioned that she had roomed with *his* mother, for a time. (She also told me how *strange* his mother had been…) I never told him that, though. I told him so many things— things I had never told *anyone*—but I also didn't tell him *everything*. I don't know if he was the same way, still guarded even for all our *honesty*. Or whether, in fact, he didn't need me *more*—didn't feel closer to *me*—than I felt towards *him*…

I needed him so much, at that time in my life. Without him, I never would have found my way out

of that *dark* place, in which I had long been stuck.
I always thought—deep down—that I didn't need
him, so much as I needed *someone*. That might have
been true, but it also forgets that *he*—that real,
individual *person*—had been the *someone* I needed.
Once again—another time in my life—I deceived
myself into thinking that I didn't care about
someone as much as I did. I was scared…

§

*(That is another way of saying that the mother, by
representing secure biological dependence, is also a
fundamental threat….)*

§

After he was gone, I would spend hours scrolling
through internet searches, trying to find any trace
of him. When I came upon a website filled with his
paintings, I visited it constantly, checking for any
updates or new paintings. (It hasn't been updated
in three years. The last painting is the saddest,
most *despairing* painting I have ever seen—because
I knew who had made it, and perhaps because (deep
down) I also knew to *expect* it…) In those moments,
wasn't I just scavenging for any remainder of that
connection—so *meaningful*—that I once had with
another person? If I missed him, though, I *deserved*
that pain, for not having admitted to myself just
how much I had *needed* him. I should have known

better, even if I was only 17 or 18, self-obsessed either through *egotism* or through *love*, and just trying—myself—to come back to life (a poor, scared *kid*), after so long being afraid to live it...

§

Years later—rereading *Denial of Death* for the umpteenth time—I noticed all these passages that had been marked, in a color of pen that wasn't familiar to me. And it wasn't familiar to me (I realized), because the markings weren't *mine*, but *his*. *His*—from when I had lent him my copy of that book (so many years ago), but had forgotten that I did so...

"But we can also see at once that there is no line between normal and neurotic, as we all lie and are all bound in some ways by lies. Neurosis is, then, something we all share; it is universal. Or, putting it another way, normality is neurosis, and vice versa. We call a man 'neurotic' when his lie begins to show damaging effects on him or on people around him and he seeks clinical help for it—or others seek it for him. Otherwise, we call the refusal of reality 'normal' because it doesn't occasion any visible problems. It is really as simple as that..."

§

The question becomes—especially now—how *similar* we really were in spirit. He clearly was further than I had thought, more in line with our *ideas*. But then have I abandoned those ideas, and run off to the safety of the *normal*, the *religious*? Did I ever really *believe* them, in the first place? M—— always knew that he was *special, great*—and he still is, even if (now) it's probably more in the form of *eccentricity (madness)*, rather than in *art*. I, too, still believe in *greatness*, but I no longer seek it in the same way I once did, neither as *forcefully*—nor as coldly *unflinching*—as our ideas would have once *demanded*. When I go to his website, isn't part of my guilt directed at me—for what *I* am—in addition to what *he* might have become? Don't I see some sort of self-recrimination in those paintings, even and especially those last and most *hopeless*? I don't think I romanticize mental illness, as I used to. But there's this sense where that should be *my* fate, too, if I was more honest. Like I am still only *playing*— as a *child* would—at this game of *greatness*, which another person actually undertook and dared to *live*. I have this *stain*, on my hands...But is it the stain of *his* life—or is it not (rather) the stain of my *own*? My own life, which I might be *wasting*— either by squandering my gifts (and my *greatness*) in the saturated and artificial numbness of the *normal*; or (what's worse) by hypocritically, *deludedly* trying to make my self into something which—as I have always known—I am *not*...

§

(In this sense, some kind of objective creativity is the only answer man has to the problem of life...)

§

Me? I have never really been an *artist*: I only *play* at it—convincing myself that I *am* one—in order to avoid the unbearable fact that I'm *not* one. Because I can't create, can't imagine, can't do anything but move around the pieces of the puzzle that *life* has already created for me. And I do all this (I write all these *words*) not in order to give forth anything deeply *true*, but just to pass the *time*, and to make my life seem more *interesting*—more *new*, more *convoluted*, and more worthy of *attention*—than the boring, all-too-clear *reflection* of me (and my *fear*). What I do, and what I write, is only a small, poor reflection—a *shadow*—of what real and great art can (and *should*) do for us. I am not an *artist*, and I never *have* been. I am (at best) the artist's *confidant*—*his* confidant. Because M—— was always the Artist, to me. And (for *better*, or for *worse*) he always will be...

§

(But did I make him into the Artist, to justify not needing to *worry* about him?)

(Or—what's worse—did I make him into the Artist, in order to keep for myself this impossible, idealized vision of *Art*?)

§

(Instinctively, as do the shipwrecked, he will look round for something to which to cling, and that tragic, ruthless glance, absolutely sincere, because it is a question of his salvation, will cause him to bring order into the chaos of his life...)

§

Why do I continually *say*—constantly *clarify*—that I am not an *artist*, that what I write isn't *art*? Isn't it because I'm *afraid* to be an artist—afraid to *fail*, perhaps; but also (perhaps more significantly) because I am afraid to accept the *consequences*, which being an artist entails? Am I simply afraid to discover just how pitiful and *imperfect* Art is, so that—even if I *was* good at it—Art wouldn't bring any deep, existential *meaning* to my life? Am I afraid to discover just how *pointless* Art is, and how it can never give me what I *want* from it: some kind of transcendent *understanding*—some type of perfect *love*—some sort of *immortality*? (*Neither greatness nor love will get you to any beyond...*) But don't I still hold onto *Art* as the hope that maybe—just maybe—it *can* get us (can get *me*) to some sort of *beyond*? Don't I still hold onto this idealized, *insane* vision of the

Artist, because I need to believe that *greatness*, or *love*, or *art* (as some unholy combination of the two) can *save* me—can get me beyond the limited, mortal circle of *myself*—in order to actually find something worthwhile, and meaningful, and *eternal*? Don't I *need* these ideas, in order to want to *live*, at all?

§

—(8:47:18PM) i feel like there's a fundamental love that my parents never gave me, and that they simply can't

— (8:48:17PM) yeh, they can never give you the happiness, the intellectual stimulation, exactly what you want

— (8:48:25PM) no one ever can except yourself

— (8:49:41PM) i disagree

— (8:49:52PM) i think some girl out there can

— (8:49:56PM) just because I said she can

— (8:50:18PM) then she exists, and hopefully you can find her

§

His *daughter*—that image he made of her—was, finally, his most honest *confession*. About how his *love* (the *Artist's* love) could only ever be realized *tomorrow*—out on that unlivable *horizon* of the unreal *future* . . . .

(Me? I always had one foot more in *reality*, satiating myself with actual hopes—for the kisses of a beautiful woman—*today*. And those *hopes*—no matter how *pathetic* and *scared* they may have been—at least kept me from blowing away...)

And that—finally—was where we diverged: the difference between an absurd hope which *foolishly*—but at least *sanely*—still strove to be *realized*, in this world; and the absurd hope, which did not want anything *here* and *now*—which had no foothold in *today*—because it was so much more *extreme* (and so much *needier*) that it had to build *castles in the sky*, if it was to *survive*, at all...

(But, finally, you can't *live* up in those castles, out on that unreal *horizon*—and you can't live down *here*, either, on this decaying *earth*—so you end up living *nowhere*, lost amongst the clouds—freezing cold and *lifeless*—surrounded only by the darkest bubbles of your own, quickly fading imagination...)

§

(And now I have this wild dream of just dropping everything, and going to Austin, and finding him, and—I don't know—*helping* him, in some way. Getting him help, apologizing for what I did, seeing for myself what was the *end* of all our words—seeing what I should really expect for *myself*, or what I must stow away (*forever*), deep and *hidden* inside myself...)

§

The *artist*—the Artist—is not a singular entity, unto himself. The Artist is *scared*, making himself into an island—idealizing *Greatness* and *Love* beyond the realms of the *possible* and the *real*—because that is the only sort of bridge (going nowhere) that he could ever dare to *build*, out from himself. *Art* can't bring him perfect *understanding* or perfect *love*, and it can't erase that deep and unforgettable *pain* which he feels—over and over and *over*—as soon as he dares to reach outward towards *anything* or *anyone*. The Artist is not just some *exceptional* individual—a super-human *quester*, endlessly searching for *perfection*, in this world—but he is, also, just as *human*, and *flawed*, and hungry for *protection*, as the rest of us. The Artist—beyond whatever grand (and *needy*) symbols we may make of him—is, in reality, just a poor, scared *child*, like we're *all* children (*poor* and *scared*), in the depths of our souls…

§

(Here we see whence the genius gets his extra burden of guilt: he has renounced the father both spiritually and physically. This act gives him extra anxiety because now he is vulnerable in his turn, as he has no one to stand on. He is alone in his freedom. Guilt is a function of fear, as Rank said…)

§

We are only *human*—closer to *worms*, than to *gods*. We are all trapped by *ourselves*—by our *illusions*, and our *fears*—kept from each other even as we most *cleave* to each other...

I should have done something for him. I should have helped him, done something—*anything*—other than puffing him up with all those ideas (about *Art* and the *Artist*), until he couldn't take them anymore (and *exploded*...)

I should have realized that I couldn't do anything, that I was a scared, stupid, *shitless* kid—himself so in need of love—but who was so closed off into *himself* that he couldn't see (couldn't *imagine*) just how much *more* someone else in the world was *suffering* and in need of *love*...

God, I should have done *anything* other than what I did—anything, at *all*—so that he would not be where he probably is right now, so that I would not be where *I* am, writing a belated *apology* (a belated *confession*, begging for forgiveness) to a person who I care so much about, and who I *hurt*, so deeply. Who that person is, though (and this is the worst part of it all), *I don't know*. I don't know if it's *him* that I am speaking to (and seeking *forgiveness* from), or whether it's *myself*. Whether it's not someone *else* (someone I will never know) who I am speaking these words to, or whether it's *him*, and *me* (and that unknown *other*), all mixed together, not any *one* of us but something *in-between*...

I wanted to write: "*Matt, if you read this—wherever you are—I hope you have found your tomorrow. Either way, I'm still waiting for you—here—today*," but I can't, because I don't know if it's *true*. I don't know *who* I am waiting for—who I am *speaking* to—who I want to rip my *heart* out for. I really don't *know*...

§

(He is truly without a family, the father of himself...)

03.15.02, 09.24.13

Je ne me connais pas du tout. (There's this scene in a novel by Rilke where the character pulls mask, after mask, after mask out of a chest, putting each one on his face...) *I don't know myself at all.* (Suddenly, he's struck by the terrible thought that there is no *end* to the masks....) *I don't know if I do love—if I have loved—if I am even* capable *of love.* (The thought that, perhaps, even his first face—his real face—is only another mask, but one which he can never pull off...) *I don't even know if I love my parents...*

§

If I am honest (and I am beginning to see—more and more—how *rarely* that is) then I could dismiss—though not easily—all the *feelings* of love that I've had. They could have merely been *lust*, or the unreal *idealization* of one individual or another. Some sort of projection-governed quest for *Greatness* or *Perfection*, which latches onto this living, breathing thing in front of me. I call that *love* (and it may be), but the love between parent and child, child and parent—that *first* love—I honestly don't know if I've ever *felt* it, at any point in my memory. I don't know if I love my parents, because I don't *feel* love for them. And I don't know if I ever *have*...

§

If you look at my behavior—especially over the long term—you wouldn't really doubt that I love my parents: the way I act with them, the gifts (of heartfelt *objects*, or piercingly blunt *words*) that I occasionally bestow on them. But all that *care*—all that *attention*—is that not (perhaps) nothing more than *habit* or *expectation*, or (perhaps) just a sort of *gratitude,* for all that they have given me? I am *tied* to my parents—*undeniably*, and *inextricably*. When (in my worst moments) it feels like a *mistake* to even have been born—when doing away with that *mistake* seems the best possible course of action—in those moments, the thought that comes to me (restraining me) is of my *parents*. How I wouldn't want them to have to *deal* with that. How I could never really do it (if I ever *really* considered doing it) until after they—*themselves*—were gone. And maybe, at that moment (after both of my parents are *dead*), I will finally know if ever really *loved* them, or not...

§

I imagine that (when my parents are *dead*) I will feel—as always—*nothing*, a *void*, towards them. But what will that *void*—that *nothing*—mean? Will it be the *void* of losing something—not unwelcome—which has figured so *much* in my life? Or will it be the heartrending *void* of losing one of the most powerful forms of love that I could ever *know*, in this world? Even if (once my parents *die*) I should *cry*, what will those *tears* be falling for: the absence of a grand, overriding *symbol*, or rather for the absence of a deep and unrelenting *love*? Even if (after my parents' *death*) I should feel an absolute *paralysis*, won't that still leave me—as always—in *doubt*: *doubt* as to whether I really love them, *doubt* as to whether I've ever loved anything—or anyone—*at all*?

§

I am perpetually dissatisfied at my own failure to *reveal* me to myself, and to know *what* and *who* I am. (*I don't know if we can pull all the masks from off our faces—I don't know if we should even* want *to...*) But in this instance—arguably the most important, and the one around which all the others revolve—it seems *best* not to know. (*Maybe the masks are there for a reason, holding us from back from what would cause more harm, and greater problems...*) Best not to know, whether I love my parents, but I can't *handle* that love. (*Perhaps causing* unforgettable *harm, and* irredeemable *problems...*) Or whether I *don't* love my parents, but I can't handle—can't *live* with—that irreparable knowledge. (*Things which we can never take back, once we've pulled all the masks from off our faces...*)

§

I don't ever really *want* to know if I love my parents (or not). For as soon as I enter into that space—in my *memory*, in my *soul*, in my *writing*—

which would be necessary to discover it, I don't know if I'll be able to find my way back out. Because I don't *want* to write about my parents, beyond purely *abstract* generalizations. I don't *want* to write about the *personal* side of the story (about March 15th, and all those times I used my silence like a *knife*, holding it out against anyone who tried to get close to me...) Perhaps there are some stories—like the story about my *parents*—that I just want to keep to *myself*. (*You secretly feel—*)

§

For if I *do* love my parents, then I will have to bear the weight of the most *intimate* and *close* connection that two beings can have, on this earth. It means that I will love them *forever* (or close to it)—even as they *age*, even as they fade *away*, even after they're *gone*. It means that I am condemned to love something that—in a sort of impossibly true logic—has to *die,* in order for me to really grow up and bring to fruition all the *love* which they have given me. As if we can only become the person they helped to make us— able to survive in this world, and to *flourish* in it, on our *own*—by no longer having them there, for us, *at all...*

§

(But if I ever did write about my parents—not for others, but for *myself*—the story would begin like this: *When I was 12 years old, my parents separated...*)

§

But if—on the other hand—I *don't* love my parents, then this knowledge would leave me constantly questioning just how much of a *human* I am, and how much of a *monster*. (And how would the story *end? With that last day...*) Such knowledge would give me certainty and freedom, yes—but the *freedom* from both *loving* and being *loved*, and the *certainty* that I wasn't even *capable* of love, at all. (*That last day, when they drove me to the bus station, saying goodbye for seven months-to-forever...*) For if I can't—don't—love my parents, those who gave me *life*, how could I ever *love* another person or another thing? (*That last day, walking up the stairs, and finding myself looking back—one last time—at them...*) How could I ever *believe* myself, if I ever were to *say* those three words—or to *feel* that perfect joy— *again? (Driving away, and finding myself—that last day—silently, invisibly sobbing...*) For doesn't it seem *best* not to know—best not to *know*, whether I love my parents—if only because I do not want to live with the *consequences*, either way? (*You secretly feel—*)

113

08.11.09, 12.17.09

My grandfather had died, the night before...

It was sudden, albeit not unexpected. (*All the months leading up to it...Receiving that phone call the last month of school...All the time spent in hospital rooms...All the time waiting for it to happen...* Knowing *that it could happen at any moment...Still feeling complete* shock *when it finally did...*)

I woke up in the sort of numb clarity that I had known many times throughout my life. My mother had left (probably to go to church, or to visit my grandmother). I was alone in the house (unless one or both of my sisters were still asleep). It had been a late night, and I didn't wake up until about ten o'clock. And—when I did—there was absolutely *nothing* in the world that I felt like doing. I ended up going for a walk, and taking music along with me. I kept on skipping over song after song, though, because (that morning) I just didn't want to listen to any of them. Finally, I came to a particular song, one which I had always enjoyed, and which seemed (that day) to fit—*perfectly*—the benumbed mood in which I found myself...

§

For the longest time, I used to tell people that I didn't listen to the lyrics of songs. That it was the *music*—the *sound* of the instruments and the voice(s)—which I paid attention to, rather than what the voices were *saying*. I heard the lyrics, of course, and I could sing along (in my head) with almost any song that I knew, anticipating the words a half-second before they appeared in the song. I even admitted—in all likelihood—that I was quite a bit *moved* (albeit unconsciously) by the lyrics of a song. But the lyrics weren't what I actively paid attention to when I listened to a song, and—if I was ever asked what I *liked* about a given song, or to express my *understanding* of it—I wouldn't talk about the lyrics, or the story, or any of that: I would only tell people (like in the case of my favorite song) that it was *sad*, *beautiful*, and *longing*, *passionate*, and *tragic*, and *alive*. In other words, I would have described it in the same way that thousands of *other* songs (and countless other works of *art*) could be described. My description would have been lacking that individuality and *distinctness* which separates one thing from another, and which shows how this song is profoundly *itself*, rather than another. The only way I really knew how to talk of music—and to share my love of it—was *wordlessly*: telling another person to go listen to a song for themselves...

§

The months after my grandfather died were also the first months that I began (the first time) to fall in love. Love—the first time I *felt* it; the first time I *said* it; the first time it was *shared*...

I don't think the one could have happened without the other—they are always so *intertwined* in my memories. It's almost like my grandfather's *death* had to happen for me to ever get to that point of *love*. Like his death was the *price* that had to be paid for my own growth into *love* and more *life*. It sounds terrible to say, but that doesn't make the feeling of it any less *true*. It's a hard *truth* (like all truths?) to admit that nothing is got for nothing, in this life. That the only way for ourselves to *grow*, is to take life from somewhere—from *someone*—else. We can *gain* only by another's *loss*—I had become *richer* in life, so what (in life) had become *poorer*?

§

I was profoundly confused by my grandfather's death. I knew what *death* was (I had certainly spent enough time thinking about it), but I still couldn't understand what—exactly—had *happened*. I knew that death was an *end* (I understood that very well), but—after it happened—I didn't understand *what* had ended, exactly. What is it that *ends* in death? What is it that we say *goodbye* to?

I do not miss him—he is not gone—I miss the life inside him...I wrote that the day after, in careful, slow letters. And it was true: he wasn't gone; he was still *there*—firmly, clearly—in my *memories*.

Don't we sometimes say that fictional characters are alive, even though they do not have *life* as we do—even though (in their world) they may be *dead*? Fictional characters are still *there*—they still *speak* to us—and it's the same for people who have died. My memories are like stories that I can revisit, forever—I can revisit Hamlet anytime I want by opening up a book, and I can revisit my grandfather anytime I want by simply opening up the book of memory. We still have a relationship—he and I— even after he's dead; that doesn't suddenly go away. My grandfather will always speak to me, his voice— so *singular* (like Hamlet's), so *indescribable*—will always sound in my ears. I'll always hear him greet me with that question—"*Whaddya say?*" (*To be or not to be?*)—for which I never had an answer. And—like always—I will have no *response*, nothing to *say*. (*The rest is silence...*) Death, then, is an *end* that takes something away from the person who has died—but it does not take that person away from *us*...

§

There were so many signs of something *new*—of a *change*, of *love*—in the months that followed. There was that essay I wrote (in broken French) about the uselessness of *regret*, when we are no longer the same person—in the past—who once *inspired* that regret. There was that long paper (about the fallibility of language, in *Much Ado about Nothing*), in which I found myself concluding—unexpectedly—that we *change*, and others *change*, and our words, themselves, *change*, so the only way to communicate is to never lose sight of those ever-*changing* conclusions. (The wonder of Shakespeare—how you can find anything in the plays, especially what you *want* to find there!) And then—finally—there was that most important of signs: being home on break, and deciding (entirely on a whim!) to let my hair grow *longer*, breaking that pattern of short, monthly haircuts which (for as long as I could remember) I had followed, unquestionably, *unthinkingly*...

Eventually, more substantial *changes* would come to my life, too. Two weeks after break, I had a girlfriend (for the first time in five years). Two months after that (my hair longer than it had ever been in my life), I said I love you for the first time. These were things that—only a few months before—I would have *doubted* I could even do. Things that I would doubted if I really *wanted*, or if I *should* want them. But *"man is a giddy thing,"* as Benedick (and Shakespeare) well knew...

§

I—clearly—*love* literature, so much. (Perhaps *too* much?) And yet (for the longest time), I seemed to completely ignore the *literary* side of music. Which is to say—the *lyrics*, the part that consists of *words*. With literature, I always try to absorb a work in its *entirety*, and I don't feel that my understanding of it is *complete*, until I've done so. Yet, with music (for so many years), I just seemed to let the *words* wash over me: searching instead for pleasing *sound*—or for momentary emotional *gratification*—without any sort of literary or holistic *understanding* taking part, either in my listening or in my appreciation.

Yet there was one song, in particular (the same song I found myself listening to, that August morning), where this incomplete *absorption* of music seemed to matter, if only a little bit. It was a song that I deeply enjoyed, and one that—in my own way, listening only to the *sound*—I also thought I *understood*: the song was *beautiful*, and *tragic*, and the fundamental feeling was—clearly—one of unremitting *sadness*. And yet, the lyrics—which I knew, and which I followed (silently) as they played in the song—didn't always reflect that feeling of *sadness*; at times, they even seemed to *contradict* it. As if there was a disconnect between the *feeling* of the music—understood purely as *sound*—and the *words* that were being sung. The lyrics were describing a break-up—something which (if I had tried to) I probably could have even put into words. But they were describing—from the perspective of the person who is leaving—why the two people *shouldn't* be together, even as the music itself (I would have staked my life on it) was full of the sadness that can only be felt by the person who has suddenly, irreparably (and *devastatingly*) been *left*.

This slight confusion didn't prevent me from *enjoying* the song, ultimately, but it did leave me with the nagging feeling—as soon as the last note faded into silence—that I was *missing* something. That—no matter how much I may have *loved* the song—I didn't completely understand *what* it was that I loved. What—exactly—*was* it, this thing that I *loved*?

§

Love (with my girlfriend) was not without its problems. (As it never is...) One night—many nights—we had a fight. I secretly loved them, even as they ripped me apart and pushed me to the brink of my limits. Like always, this fight was basically just our own insecurities (hidden behind our *words*) threatening to tear us apart. (*How can you love, when love means completely opening yourself up—and thus giving yourself completely away—to another person?*) (*How can we love each other now, when, in a month from now, in a year from now, after all the changes we undergo and with the ebbs and flows of our feelings, it's possible—probable—likely—that our love will be gone?*) (Or, as I'd put it more clearly— afterwards—for both of us: *How can you love that which is going to die?*)

We left it half-resolved, at best. It was exam week (I was busy finishing a paper on Nietzsche), and we were both in need of *sleep*—and time *apart*—in order to get everything done. She left me, though, with a question, one which—more than any other (both then and now)—I had no answer to. (*What do you want?*)

§

I had probably been listening to that particular song—always with that same, nagging feeling—for about three years, before greater *understanding* suddenly came to me: without warning (*It was sudden, albeit not...*) and without seeking for it...

There are moments in life when our skin feels more deeply the slight *chill* of the wind. (The lyrics of the song formed a *letter*—one written *to* the singer, to the person who has been *left*...) Moments—in life—when the sunlight seems to make the colors of everything so much *brighter*. (A *letter*—talking about why they shouldn't be *together*, how you *hold me down*...) Moments when music suddenly sounds so much more *clearer*, than it ever has before. (How their relationship isn't *good* for either of them, no matter how much they still *love* each other...) Moments when—for the first time—you're really *hearing* a song, and hearing the *words*...

The song was so much *sadder*, that August morning—listening to the lyrics, and really *hearing* them—than it ever had been, before. It was also more *real*. For me, it was infinitely more heartbreaking to know that the lyrics were a *letter*— written by a departed lover—and now being read (the next morning) by the one who has, irreparably, been *left*. "*How will I break the news to you?*" the singer repeats (in absolute *agony*) at the end of the song, bashing his head—against these *words*—over and over and over, again…

§

That night (after our fight), I had a dream. I'm still not sure (to this day) if I interpreted it correctly—but that didn't matter. What mattered (when I awoke, the next morning) was that I wrote her a long text—spanning three messages—telling her what I *wanted*. What I wanted was *her*—what I wanted was *love*—and I was ready for whatever that *love* demanded: opening myself up *completely*, giving myself *away* completely, *hazarding* myself, risking *death*, *changing*, *anything*, anything at *all*…

§

My mother and I had gone over, after we got the call. I remembered (the next morning, looking back on it) being in my grandparents' living room, and sitting on the organ bench, where—since I was young—I had always sat, whenever we visited. I was trying not to look straight ahead—into the other room—because that was where my grandfather's body was. I didn't remember feeling sad that night, sitting on that organ bench, having already seen the body. I remembered feeling angry: helplessly, piteously *angry*. I kept asking myself—over and over again— *Is this all we're condemned to: blindness and death?* Is this all we have to look forward to, in life: a terrible and inevitable movement towards *death*, preceded by a deep and unknowing *blindness* towards everything else? (*Blindness and Death, Blindness and Death...*) How we have this deep, *willful* aversion to looking at our lives honestly—not only how they *end*, but how they *begin*, and everything in between. How we see so obscurely—and incompletely—the realities of our lives, because we don't *want* to see them, and it's only after tremendous, *piercing* events—things which are so real, that we *can't* ignore them—that we come to see our lives at all *truthfully*, seeing how *blind* we are the rest of the time. We are condemned to *blindness* about ourselves, until those brief moments of clarity when our blindness recedes and we suddenly see our lives for what they *are*—which only come to us with *death*. We can have only *blindness* or *death*, *blindness* or *death*—is that the impossible choice of our (irreparable) *fate*?

§

A few nights later (the last night we would be together, for a month), she gave voice—for the only time that I remember—to those *fears* about love that had always been haunting her: *How could love be what we feel it must be, when it is all too likely that you will change, or the other will change, and your love will one day become just another interest or fashion that you have—now—outgrown?*

(Like life, love is not permanent and unchanging. People in love are continually changing, continually moving towards and away from each other. We only think that love—and life—are *permanent*, because we want and *need* them to be. As if we built up this image of love as perfect and *unchanging*, because we could not deal with the lingering possibility that always lies underneath, waiting. Love demands the continual effort of two people who come *back* to each other—*love* each other—again and again, over and over, for as long as the love lasts. The only way to love—the only way that, in reality, we *do* love—is not as *permanence* (as our fear had taught us), but through *change*, through our own, *willed* change, over time...)

To love means to forever want to catch up to another person, to forever want to know and meet them again and follow their life through their changes and stay with them, with them in their changes, through it all...

§

For a moment, she was silent. Then she gave me this strange look, which I could never describe, and could never forget. She said it was like everything had changed, like everything was completely *different*. Or: like everything was the same, but she was *seeing* it, for the first time...

(What did she mean?) At the time, I thought I knew what these words—*her* words—meant, but now I am no longer sure. Or: I did know what they meant to her (*then*), but I'm not sure what—if anything—they still mean to her, *now*...

(Later that night, she would also give the best description of me that I have ever found: "*so pure...*" Maybe I was so *pure*, then. Maybe—when she left—she would take that *purity* away. Or—maybe—nothing has changed...)

§

Later, our love would grow old and die. (As all things do...) My insecurities—the words of my *fear*—too, would soon reveal the flaws, the *incompleteness*, they had always carried. (It's not only: *How can you love that which is going to die?* But also: *How can you love at all, being* yourself *something that is going to die?*) Because it was really me who had changed, and who brought about the end. She was finicky and tempestuous—a rather *giddy* thing—and that didn't help. But I didn't blame her. Love had become a *weight* to me—which it shouldn't be, not when we are ready and willing to love, in spite of anything. I wasn't ready for that full and open love—I wasn't prepared to *live* with it—past those couple days we still spent together. (*What do you want?*) It would take a few weeks, but slowly, inevitably, I began to change, and the fear of the *future*—of the *end* of our *love*—began to eat away at me, and to consume our love itself. It was like I had fallen out of love. Not that I didn't still have *feelings* for her—I still did (and I still would, for far too long...) Rather that—for the next two months—I could no longer bear what I knew love *was* and had to *be,* could no longer *want* to reach out, after another...

(There is a shadow surrounding every moment of our lives that—if we looked at it long enough—would profoundly *terrify* us: the fact that who we are in *one* moment, is not who we are in the *next*. But that *change*—of course—could be from *here* to *there*, from *happy* to *sad*, or from *love* to *not-love*, just as well as it could be from *life* to *death*, or from *sound* to *silence*...)

§

Hamlet—the *Prince of Denmark*—the only individual (real or otherwise) who I still try to *emulate*, in my life. Of course, there was another person (who *was* real) who I used to look up to, in life—but he's no longer around, except in memory. I can't go to him—can't ask him *advice*, can't *talk* to him—because (like Hamlet) though he might not be *gone*, there's nothing there (no *life*) to interact with. The dead (like my grandfather) may be similar to literary characters, in that they always *remain*; but then—also like literary characters—they can never truly *change*, not anymore. What their story *was*, is what their story always will *be*, since the author—in both cases—has written no more. (*The rest is...*) The *relationship* with the person may not die when the person does, but what remains is a pale shadow of that *life*—that living *connection*—which once was, between you. What your connection *was*—with that person, in the past—is what it always shall be: *now*, and *forever*. (*Whaddya say?*)

Even if I knew that my grandfather always greeted me in the same way—even if I could picture, with almost perfect clarity, what he would *look* like and *sound* like—there would still be something *missing*. (*I'll always hear him greet me with that question, that question for which I never had an answer...*) Because, even if I did—even if, finally, I understood what that question *meant* and how to *answer* it (that question which had nagged me for so many years, and which—when I knew it was coming—made me *shrink* up into myself, because my *words* had deserted me)—even if I did know how to respond to that question, *now*, I couldn't, not *anymore*. My grandfather may be able to speak to *me*—in my *memory*—but I can no longer speak to *him*. If he remains, it's as a ghost—someone who *I* can see—but who doesn't really see *me*...

Ultimately—at the center of ourselves—we are *nothing*. *Death* will come. Life is a *dream*, from which we will one day *awake*. My grandfather is *dead*, and nothing can change that. He is not *gone*, and he will not be gone until all memories of him fade. But then I, too, will eventually be *dead*—no longer able to *remember* him, or *speak* to others, or have new *experiences*, or *change*. I—too—will eventually be *gone*, when the last echo of my voice finally disappears from the cosmos. (*Whaddya say?*)

§

That August morning—after my grandfather's death—hearing that particular song as if for *the first time*...it was perfect, and listening to it was probably the only way I could let myself express (in any form) the *pain* that I hadn't yet begun to acknowledge. Of course, it was a song I had greatly enjoyed—and now, even, one that I *loved*—but the *love* I had for it was far less than the *love* I had for my grandfather, now gone. Fittingly, it was only when I already had all the pain I could imagine, that another, deeper part of the song—the poignant, elegiac truth of *words*—finally came to me. After all, what's a little *more* pain, when we already have too *much*? (*I know I love you because I miss you all the time...*)

§

The funeral was a few days later. Afterwards, we went back to my grandparents'—now only my grandparent's—house. Once again (like always), I sat down on the organ bench. But this time, for some reason—perhaps just to find something to occupy my hands—I turned around and started to play. I didn't know how, apart from all the half-hearted notes that I had played on it, when I was younger. (*Played* on it—like a children's *game*, not like *music*...) But there were notes $(A^b, C^\#)$ written both on the page and on the keys themselves, so that—with my meager musical background—I could manage, well enough. (It was mostly religious songs that I had to choose from, so I also knew—at least—how they were supposed to *go*...) After playing a piece a few times—at half-speed, and with not infrequent mistakes—I eventually succeeded in playing a passably familiar (and passably pleasing) version of several songs. Yet I made sure to play *softly*, since everyone in the living room (after the difficulty of the past few days) had fallen asleep. Later, I found out that some people (my mother, my aunts, and my grandmother, who were cleaning up in the kitchen) could also hear the music. (When, afterwards, they told me how *nice* it had been, I remained—graciously?, disbelievingly?—*silent*...)

At the time, though, I didn't know that. I didn't know that they (or anyone) could hear me, as I played. And I didn't know that anyone—any living soul—was listening, when (for some reason) I began to play, over and over and over again, the same, particular song. It was a song that was normally *sung*, of course, and one that was full of *words*. And yet, at that moment, the only thing I heard was the *voice* of the organ—singing (*wordlessly*) the melody—as it began avoiding sharp *breaks*, skipping over *entrances* and *exits*, refraining from all abrupt *beginnings* and jarring *endings* (which might wake someone up), simply striving for a continual flow of *music* that could cover over the silence (*the rest*), always waiting patiently, at the end...

Losing an illusion...

"Losing an illusion makes you wiser than finding a truth."

– Ludwig Börne

I do not know if I agree with that quote...

The first time I read it (when I was 17), I thought that finding a *truth* was more important, and I argued—passionately—against those who agreed with Mr. Börne. Now, though, I'm less and less sure. If anything, I am currently more partial towards ridding ourselves of our *illusions*—so many and so impenetrable—than of trying to find something that we can call *truth*. Yet—admittedly— *truth* would seem so fragile and so rare a thing, that we should cherish it like an unrepayable *gift*, when and if it does ever come to us...

§

Twelve Angry Men—a movie filmed by Sidney Lumet in 1957—swirls around the question of *illusion* and *truth*, carrying us between the two through a movement of questioning and doubt. The story is simple: twelve jurors are placed together in a jury room, in order to decide the conviction or acquittal of a young man accused of having murdered his father. The plot, too, is simple. At the beginning, all twelve jurors take a preliminary vote, and all but one vote for conviction. Throughout the rest of the movie, this lone Juror—#7—begins to unravel the prosecutor's argument and exhibit all the holes in what seemed to everyone else an open-and-shut case. As the movie progresses, each of the jurors—one by one—changes their votes, until, at the end, the jury unanimously agrees to return a verdict of "*not guilty*."

Juror #7 does not seem to bring the other jurors to his side by swaying them with any *truth*, though— he only repeats (again and again) that "*It's possible*" that the defendant is innocent, insisting that there is enough reasonable *doubt* as to warrant further examination of the case. By continually putting forth new possibilities, Juror #7 progressively chips away at the hard truth of "*guilty*" that the other jurors had held about the case, revealing all those personal prejudices and *illusions* that each and every juror— inevitably—brought into the deliberation room. Some of the jurors are swayed by the evidence, which is not as airtight as had first appeared in court. Others—in considering the skewed, unflattering narrative told about the defendant— were prejudiced against the neighborhood and the environment in which he grew up. One of the jurors is a bigot, who eventually comes to admit the unthinking bias that was guiding his vote for guilty.

The last juror to be swayed has also been the most hostile throughout the deliberation, adamantly on the side of the "*guilty*." The climactic moment occurs when the real reason for his stubborn refusal comes to light, and everyone learns that his personal feelings towards his own, estranged son have entirely clouded whatever judgment he had towards the trial in question.

In some sense, what wins out in the end is *doubt,* rather than *truth.* It is doubt that reveals and relieves all of the jurors of all their personal *illusions,* and it is doubt that leads them to discover enough *reasonable doubt,* so as to finally put forth a verdict of "*not guilty*." Does that mean—ultimately—that the defendant didn't do it? (Not necessarily...) "*Not guilty*" does not have to mean "*innocent,*" though it may mean that. Technically, it only has to mean that the *truth* of "*not-guilty*" was strong enough to withstand the doubt which was directed towards it by the prosecution. Ultimately, the final verdict means—quite simply—there was a greater *probability* of "*not guilty*" over "*guilty,*" *innocence* never coming into the picture.

Yet—in the end—the movie does not seem to follow this *doubt* to its furthest conclusions. Unlike the original play from which the movie is adapted, there is an added scene—at the very beginning of the film—before we have even entered the deliberation room and met the individual jurors. Passing through shots of the stately, *imposing* courthouse—with its large white columns, and majestic, bustling halls— we enter the courtroom just as the judge gives his final directions to the jurors. Right at the end—as the jurors are leaving the courtroom—we see a shot of the defendant: an extremely young man, sitting alone at a table, who appears strained—perhaps nervous or scared—with his large eyes seemingly reddened by some sort of worry or anxiety. In those few seconds, I (at least) am drawn to feeling *sympathy* for him; and—if the viewer had to make a judgment, right then—I imagine that *"innocent"* would far outweigh *"guilty."* For it's not *"guilty"* or *"not guilty"* that we feel when we look at this young man, sitting in a courtroom, waiting for his *fate* to be decided—it's *innocence* or *culpability*. It's a definite *truth*—one way or the other—that we're disposed to assert.

It's clear that such inclinations or feelings should not have a foremost—if *any*—place in a courtroom. But such feelings are the stuff of decision and the basis for *action*, when what we need is not a probability achieved through *doubt*, but a strong *belief*, one way or the other. Would they have acquitted the defendant, if they didn't think he was *innocent*? Would a higher probability of *"not guilty"* convince them to let a possible murderer go free, when doing so could endangers others' lives, or their own? Could someone sleep soundly at night, having made a life-or-death decision based solely on *doubt*?

Ultimately, the question around which the movie turns is whether the verdict—decided on by the twelve jurors—argues for the *truth* of the young man's *innocence*, or only the *truth* of his *non-guilt*. Can we assert the latter, without also believing the former? Judicially, we can separate *"guilt"* and *"non-guilt,"* without ever speaking of *innocence*. But pragmatically—in real *life*—it's so much grayer and less clear. The judicial system seems to depend on *doubt*, instead of *truth*—where there's *"reasonable doubt"* as to one's guilt; or, lacking that, where there remains a proof of guilt *"beyond a reasonable doubt."* Yet the reality of the situation—and of *action*—always depends on *truth*, rather than *doubt*. When it comes time to act—when we must make a decision that will have *consequences*, out in the world—*doubt* often disappears, and for good reason. Are we willing to consummately follow the path of *doubt*, if it means that we—or our loved ones—might, one day, meet a wrongly-acquitted murderer in the street?

Suppose that—in fact—Juror #7 really has no predispositions one way or another, neither believing in the defendant's *innocence* nor in his *guilt*. He simply recognizes the opposing possibility of *innocence* that has been so overshadowed by the prosecutor's case, and urges the other jurors to spend more time examining it. Suppose that this dedication to *doubt* and questioning leads—finally—to a more thorough and unprejudiced consideration of the case as a whole, such that sufficient *"reasonable doubt"* has emerged to convince the other jurors of an acquittal. Yet what has he swayed them to? When they vote *"not guilty,"* it is not simply the presence of an unrelenting *doubt* that they are affirming. In practical matters of the real world, they are affirming (at the very least) the higher *probability* of the defendant's *innocence*, a probability sufficiently great to lead them to affirm—with *certainty*—his *innocence* over his *"guilt."* Because—without this certainty—they would have to live with the deeply unsettling consequences of letting someone potentially *guilty* walk free. Or (what may be worse) of sentencing an *innocent* man to *death*.

Of course, one could argue that the evidence in the case is not only highly *probable*, but *"beyond all reasonable doubt,"* providing a firm enough foundation upon which to make a final decision. But the evidence is *"beyond all reasonable doubt"* for what—the defendant's *"innocence,"* or only for his *"non-guilt"*? What I am trying to show, is that there is a *disconnect* between the decisions we make, and the ways we arrive at those decisions. No matter how thoroughly we adhere to *doubt* and remain in the realm of *"reasonable"* possibilities, a *truth* inevitably sneaks in and influences us one way or the other, according to the prejudices—and *illusions*—of which we can never (no matter how hard we *try*) rid ourselves. If the jurors believed he was *innocent*, then they left behind—of necessity—the *doubt* that brought them to such *truth*. And, even if the jurors simply followed the path of *doubt*—all the way to its conclusion—there would still be demanded of them that personal *signature* which chooses to favor one possibility over others. We still have to assert that which—to *us*—seems most probable, thereby agreeing to live—for the rest of our lives—with the consequences of both our *actions* and our *beliefs*.

Let us return to Juror #7. Imagine that—before him—are all those facts that seem to bespeak the defendant's *innocence*, such that *"reasonable doubt"* has been attained and the probabilities favor acquittal rather than conviction. But also before him is something that he cannot banish from his thoughts, because it was that which first lead both him and the jury to their decision: namely, that *doubt*—that lingering sense of possibility—which has been the driving force of the movie. He might exit the courthouse, smiling and confident in his decision, but there always remains the possibility that maybe, just maybe, he was wrong—and thus that the entire jury was wrong, as well. Perhaps even he, ultimately, is acting upon assumptions or personal inclinations—personal *illusions*—when *doubt* leaves open several, opposing possibilities. Perhaps, for Juror #7, these inclinations make him tend towards a belief in the fundamental *goodness* of humanity—as if he were willing to believe the best of people, when the evidence for acquittal (though probable) still does not give him certainty or *truth*, one way or the other[9]. This belief in the *goodness* of humanity largely buttresses him against the most dreadful thoughts—of letting a *murderer* go free—as it does for many of us, in the actions and decisions that we make each day. Yet this belief which guides him is just as much uncertain *prejudice* and unfounded *illusion* as anything else. Painful though the recognition may be, there is sufficient evidence—throughout *history*, and in our own *world*—to claim that humanity is not, inherently, *good*. Which is not to deride the belief that it *is*, but

9 Consider, too, the charge itself: a young man murdering his father. In returning a verdict of *"not guilty,"* the jurors decide that the defendant—the *son*—has not killed his *father*. Which is to say, in a symbolic sense, that *tradition*—and what has come *before* us—is upheld. We hold onto *tradition* and to the *past*, when it had something useful or *good* in it; we oppose it when it no longer suits us, or has proven itself *corrupted*. Deciding that the son has not killed the father further strengthens (perhaps) the movie's subtle inclination towards the fundamental *goodness* of humanity, that unimpeachable *goodness* which is passed down, from one generation to another…

simply to recognize the true meaning of what it is to *believe* and to have *faith*, in circumstances where certainty and *truth* will not—and cannot—be found. (*You don't let me play the victim...*)

I can imagine an extra scene at the end of the movie—after the jurors have left the courthouse, and are returning home—when the camera momentarily stops on a shot of the courthouse stairs. I envision a young man (the defendant) stepping out of the courtroom, alive and free like he never thought he would be again. He descends the staircase (as the others jurors have done) and walks through the streets, until he comes to a door in an apartment building. He opens the door and goes inside what (evidently) must be his home. He walks over to the window, or perhaps to a given spot in the room, and suddenly he flashes back to a scene with a man, and a knife, and he's stabbing, stabbing, stabbing (this man, his *father*). The scene ends when we see Juror #7, sitting up in his bed (breathing hard, pale or covered in sweat), and staring into the darkness with a look of *anguish* on his face—like one who has just awoken from a terrible dream...

We need our *faiths*—our *illusions* of *truth*—to support our actions. But where certain *truth* is absent, no possibility (no matter how *dark*) ever disappears...

04.18.13, 09.23.12

Je suis le personne le plus indépendant du monde...

I was coming back from a tiring, twelve-day trip through southern Europe, spent largely with one of my sisters. (I first visited Florence—alone—and then traveled with her to Rome, Barcelona, and Madrid...) I had gotten back to a small town about 12 km (8 miles) from my own, and—since there was no direct connection, between the two—I tried calling someone who (before the trip) had offered to pick me up. (Offered, of her *own* accord—I never would have called her, otherwise...) For some reason, though, my phone wasn't working. Or, my calls weren't getting through. Or, she—quite simply—wasn't picking up. And so, even though it would mean 8 miles of walking—8 miles, along narrow, *winding* roads, not made for pedestrians; 8 miles, carrying a rather large, *heavy* backpack; 8 miles, on a dark, hazy afternoon, which would soon turn into *rain*—even knowing all that (oh, the deep resonance of the scene!), I started walking...

I tried calling her several more times, as I walked, but she didn't answer, and I wouldn't—I just *wouldn't*—consider calling anyone else. *The world would be better—easier—if everyone just took more care of* themselves; *and, if you can't get something* yourself, *then you should just learn to live* without *it.* (That, at least, is how I would have expressed it, several years earlier...) As I walked, I even thought about hitchhiking—asking one of the people who I passed in the town (or on the road) if they wouldn't mind driving me the ten minutes further along. But I didn't—I was stubbornly refusing to ask for help—because I would rather have *died* doing what I was doing (*YOU'RE BATSHIT INSANE!*), than dare to depend on anyone other than *myself*...

The next day, I was sick. For me, though, illness is never purely *physical*—there's always a *spiritual* element, as well, infecting not only my *head* or my *throat*, but my *mind*, my *feelings*, my *thoughts*, and my *soul*. That day, I finally looked at what I had put off looking at, before leaving for my trip—the results of the Quidditch World Cup, the first one (in four years!) that had taken place without me. (*Why had I put it off?*) Because—as I said to myself—I didn't *care*, anymore. (*But really?*) Or—rather—it was because I still cared too *much*, about something that wasn't *mine* to care about, anymore. I felt better over the course of the day—in my body—but, unlike other times, no *insight*, no saving *resolution*, came to quell the dark thoughts spinning in my head. It was only a few days later—settled back into my slightly strange home, my job for the year ended, and with nothing to look forward to but 80 days of trying, finally, to be a *writer*—it was only then (after a dream) that a sort of *realization* finally came into my thoughts. This time, though, it wasn't a *pleasant* realization, not one that *freed* me—or *opened* up the future—for greater *love* or more *life*. This realization wasn't like that, because (on the one hand) it spoke entirely of the *past*, and (on the other) because it was the most *painful* that I had experienced, in my recent memory:

I ended it because I was scared...

§

(I've always known, without having to question myself at all, that our relationship had an expiration date. Not that we might not one day end up together again, but that it had to end—to truly and utterly end—in order for our love to be what it always was, what it always would be...)

We agreed to end it when I left. I knew enough—about *life*, about *love*, and about *time;* about *her*, and about *myself*—to know that we should end it. That it would be for the best—for *both* of us—to break it off...

(All that is born must die, and all that loves must end, and the unavoidable fact of life is that time passes, and things change, and there's nothing you can ever do to stop it or alter it, death only being another step in that ever changing process...)

For didn't I know—after being with her for six months—that we (both of us) would have been absolute *wrecks*, if we tried to hold it together?

Didn't I know—hadn't I *learned*, from experience—that long-distance relationships (when life is pulling you in different directions) aren't a good idea, and that the fixity they demand (holding onto something so far from your own life) wouldn't be good for *anyone's* growth or development?

(*But one that did not end for anything except time, except for the unavoidable fact of change in life, because I will be moving on in life and going to France and you will be here, and the lines which our lives draw over the face of the globe will greatly diverge for an extended period of time, no matter how much we might try to keep them close...*)

Wasn't it a sort of *maturity* that was telling me to end it—telling me *not* to try holding onto something, no matter how much you may *love* it—when that thing wouldn't be *good* (for either of you), anymore?

(*I wanted so much to give you love, but I also knew that the best way I could do that, would be also to one day to give you the pain of losing love. They go together, and they always will...*)

And wasn't it a sort *wisdom*—no matter how *painful* that wisdom may have been—which had been telling me (over and over, again and again) to *end* it, that it *had to* end, that ending it would be for the *best*?

(That love would make you better, finally, even if that meant hours and days and weeks and months of pain...)

I had never thought differently, had never considered otherwise, had never questioned that *wisdom*, because I knew (I *knew*, in my heart of hearts) that this was what the way it had to be, that we had to break it—our *love*—off...

(All love will break you, inevitably...)

But what if that wasn't—totally—*true?* What if that wasn't—really—true, *at all?* What if it hadn't been *wisdom*, or *maturity*, or the memory of all those bitter *lessons* that I had learned, which was telling me to end it? Perhaps, yes, it *had* been all those things, as I had always believed. But perhaps—*perhaps*—it had been something worse, darker, and more *afraid*, there at the very center. Perhaps it had been fear—*fear*—the whole time: *fear*, masquerading as wisdom and maturity; *fear*, hiding under the costumes of beautiful words and wise sentiments; fear—*fear*—which had inspired everything I had said, and everything I had done, when *I—myself,* and my *fear*—had ended it...

(I ended it because I was scared...)

No more lies or half-truths—we've had enough of those for a lifetime. It was *me* who ended it, and I ended it out of *fear*. And I didn't *realize* that—didn't admit it to *myself*—for seven months...

§

(I never once questioned the inevitability of the *end*. I never brought it up. I never mentioned the possibility—the *hope*, because *who knows?*—of continuing past that definite end-date that had been set. And she only brought it up *once*, at the end...)

Throughout all that time, I had *cleaved* to the end, as if it was a good thing. I *lauded* it, heaped upon it so much meaning and *significance*, because— for me—that *end* had made our *love* what it was. That *end* had made our love *possible*, since—without the end of the school year, lingering in sight—I never would have *said* anything, at all. (*And how it might have just ended at that, with nothing more, except a silent and unsent letter, to myself...*) Then, later, that *end* had always made me *run after her*, instead of just letting her go. (That first night—after we had hugged each other and departed—but I kept walking around and around in pointless, indecisive *circles*, trying to decide whether or not to go back and *kiss* her...) That *end* had always made me dig *deeper*—and try *harder*—because there was so little *time* left for us. (That fateful night—at the end of the year—when it would have been so *easy* just to let her go, after she had stormed out of the room and (like a *child*) wouldn't even *answer* me...) That *end* had determined the entire character of our relationship, and—if it was a *limit*—then it was also the defining *feature* of our *love* (*What if we tried?*), the one that suffused everything we did, and said, and thought, and *felt,* towards each other. (*What if. What if. What IF?*)

§

(But that *end* also gave me the excuse to hold something *back* in love—not to love her as much as I *could* have, not to love her *fully*, not to imagine a *future* with her, not to allow myself to rush after her *forever…*)

I was the one who held fast to the end-date, and never questioned it, and never let myself hope or dream of a *future*, beyond September 23rd. It was like the date had been set in stone—I couldn't *erase* it, so I never thought to *question* it. I *felt*—inside myself— that it had to end, and I never wavered from that *feeling*. This was simply the way it *was*—the way it had to *be*—and I didn't even need to *think* about it to know that. It *had* to end—it was *going* to end—and all we could do was enjoy it while it lasted, inventing beautiful-sounding phrases (*All that is born must die, and all that loves must end…*), to try to make that *end* seem less horrible *(But one that did not end for anything except time, except for the unavoidable fact of change in life…)*

§

146

(Really, though, it was not *life*—or *time*—that brought about the end, but me, *myself*. And I would have *seen* that, if I hadn't been too scared to simply— honestly—*look* at myself. Too *scared*, to simply— honestly—*end* it...)

That unquestioned *fixation* on the *end* prevented me from seeing what I—*myself*—was really doing: all those thoughts, actions, and decisions, so deeply influenced by my *fear*. My *fear* spoke to me in all these words of *wisdom*, these things which *self-reflection* had taught me over the years. *Time changes us...Love comes and goes...All that lives must die... Only the end can inspire us...*I carried these ideas like *scars*: to remind me of what I had been through (the first time, two years ago), and to never forget those *painful*—but *vital*—lessons which I had learned. But—from May to September—these ideas became distorted, *grotesque*. As if all that I had gained through self-reflection—self-*knowledge*, powerful *insights*, honest *sentiments*, beautiful *words*, deep *thoughts*, *wisdom*—had been turned *against* me, by the clever schemes and manipulations of my *fear*. Perhaps—at times—my *words* can be *beautiful*. (Well, then *Beauty* might be the most lying and deceptive *bitch* that I have ever met, in my life...) Perhaps my *thoughts*— at least—*strive* towards honesty. (But aren't the most *honest*-seeming—so often—the most *hypocritical?*) Perhaps—ultimately—I *do* aspire towards *wisdom*, in life. But *wisdom*—ultimately—may not even be worth the shirt on our *backs*. (That, at least, keeps us *warm*, instead of making us *colder*—and more *hesitant*—to go out into the world...)

§

Before leaving for Paris, two years ago (that same semester I *meditated* and tried to be *empty*), I took a class on the English Romantic poets. The text we primarily focused on that semester was Wordsworth's long, autobiographical poem, *The Prelude*. In it, Wordsworth describes his life—from his earliest memories, up to the present moment in which he's writing—showing how he became who he was, but also (more deeply) how he always had *been* who he one day *became*. In particular, it was while reading the section on the French Revolution that I had one of the most memorable *artistic* experiences of my life. When the Revolution first begins, it inspires Wordsworth to an *unprecedented* height, carrying all his *hopes* and *dreams,* and representing—for him—the highest ideal of what *could* be, suddenly made *real*. (Throughout the course—no matter how much I may have seemed to *agree* with them—I was fighting a silent, fervent battle *against* the Romantics...) But then, when the Revolution begins to turn—becoming instead a slaughter of human *life*, of *justice*, of *innocence*, and of all the *ideals* that it had ever carried for him— then Wordsworth *broke* down, in a way I that could never mimic in writing, not in a thousand years. (I was fighting—above all—against their eternal, *indestructible* vision of *hope*, even after all that they had been through...) It would take a long time—demanding much suffering—for Wordsworth to get out of the impossible *depression* into which he had fallen. (*He left behind the woman he loved, and their unborn child...*) He had to learn to *live,* again, not just with the terrible *realities* of all that had happened in France, but with the terrible reality—now destroyed, now *dead*—of all the *hopes*, *dreams*, *wishes*, and *visions* that he had once made, for *life*, itself. (*No matter what visions I might have, no matter what beautiful imaginings enter your head, we can't hold on to something already dead...*)

§

All love should end in a beautiful birth... That was another one of those *wise* sayings that I kept repeating—to *her*, and to *myself*—to try to make the end seem less *horrible*. For me, all I could do was hope that our *end*—for whatever pain and *suffering* it would (inevitably) bring—might also lead, in some sense, to a beautiful *birth*. At the time, I thought that would be as a sort of *rebirth*, for each of us—passing through *death*, and eventually coming back to *life*—both stronger and more ready to *live* (and to *love*), again.

But (at the end) I also found myself making up this strange *image*—this metaphor of a *child*—that we had had, together. As if our relationship itself were this beautiful, *living* thing, one which—together—we had once *created* and given *birth* to. *(And it was so beautiful because it was so alive: thrown into the world, with such highs of joy and lows of pain, and alive enough even to die, as all things do…)*

§

Two years ago (at the end of my stay in Paris), I had a sequence of three dreams…

In the first dream, I simply walked away, leaving behind the *pregnant* woman—the mother of my *child*—whom I loved…

The second dream was a poem (composed almost entirely in my sleep) by a father whose *child*—seemingly—has *died*. The poem itself is a note, left behind for his wife (*"Judith, give this to my unborn child"*), because he can't stand to stay there—with her, and with their *loss*—anymore. (*"But all I have are these poor words/So take them with patience and with pity…"*)

The last was a dream-story (written in the third person) in which the main character—an army officer—is recollecting an experience he once had *"After the war…"* In the memory, he watches as his general—in a rage—*screams* at a woman, one who (he is convinced) is a *traitor*, and has just cost thousands of men their lives. She is standing there—along with her three children—when the general (trying to get her to *confess*) puts a gun to one of their heads. She doesn't confess, though—she *pleads* with him—and he shoots one child, and then the second, and then the third. The general walks away, and the main character (in his memory) sees before him this utterly *devastated* woman—this *mother*. (*He bent down to pick up the pistol that had buried itself in the snow and wiped it clean with his handkerchief...*) He hears one of the other soldiers—an old man—say to him: "*It would be crueler now not to do it...*" (*He aimed it towards its target, a victim completely aware of her fate, a woman shaking uncontrollably as she stared at the bodies of the three children she had just seen slain before her...*) The recollection soon ends. (*He closed his eyes...*) The main character is back in the present, and—in a response to a woman, who has just asked him what happened to *the mother and children*—he says (simply), "*They all died...*" In his mind, though, he is imagining—since, in reality, *He had turned and never looked back*—what that scene would have looked like, afterwards:

four bodies sprawled out on a sheet of bloodied snow in the middle of a silent wood...

It was a strange and beautiful dream, at least for me. (And a better story than I could ever have written, when awake...) If the story and the dream—and all *three* dreams—has any *truth*, though, then

I was the one who killed them. (*The mother and children...*) For—in *reality*—hadn't I killed *her* (the woman I loved), and hadn't I also killed our *child* (our relationship, our *love*) *itself?*

§

(When you break up, something in your life, some part of you, is missing, gone, essentially as if it disappeared or has died. But you do not die, and the other person does not die (usually), so what is it that you are mourning and crying for? In the aftermath of a break-up, you go on living your life, and the other person goes on living their life, but you both feel as if you've lost something, something precious and irreplaceable. That something is the relationship itself, this child which you've created and watched grow up, nourished and cared for and now have to bury...)

If only I could have imagined it when it was still alive! (I thought to myself—so often— afterwards...) *If only I could have loved this—our child—as a loving parent should, instead of being the one who had brought about its death!* Because it was *me—I* was the one—who had killed our child, because I had been too *scared* to love it. I was too scared to *love* it, too scared to take *care* of it, too scared to have the responsibility of *raising* it, too scared to have to watch it grow *up*, and *change*, and *live*, and then—ultimately—to also have to watch it *die*, as if it had never *existed*. (*How can you love that which...*)

I couldn't truly love our *child* (or *any* child) because I couldn't stop myself from constantly imagining its *death*—its own, inevitable *end*—as well as all the *pain* and *suffering* which it would experience, along the way. For—ultimately—wasn't our *child* (our *love*) already *dead*, as soon as it was *born*? Hadn't we *killed* it, even as we brought it into *existence*? Doesn't begetting *life* also mean—irreparably—begetting *death*? (*And so I leave...*)

§

I couldn't handle the weight of that *love*—the weight of being a *parent*. And so I left. So I killed our relationship—our *child*—by letting it *die*, pretending that it had always been fated to die at that moment, and there was *nothing* I could do to stop it. Really, though, that was just the way I tried to *escape* (leaving the child *behind*, simply walking *away*) my own, intolerable *fear*. It's one thing to try to love someone *fully*, and with all your *heart*. It's another thing to give *birth* to something, to take *care* of it, to *raise* it—to give your whole *life* to it—knowing (the whole time) that it only can live through the unqualified *love* that you have for it. Knowing that—as soon as your *love* begins to *waver* or *fade*—they, too, will *waver*, *fade*, and *disappear*, and there's nothing (*nothing*) that you can do to stop it. It was our *love*—the love of each *other*, the love of our *child*—that had kept our relationship alive. But I couldn't bear the weight

153

of such *selfless* love—the love of being a *parent*. I couldn't bear that highest *affirmation* of everything, of *life* itself—giving *birth*, and then being able to *love* (completely, unequivocally, *unconditionally*) this new, living, and *dying* creation...

I thought I was over her four times, when (all the while) I was deeply—depressingly—*not* over her…

There was that moment—after less than a week—when (thinking of her) I felt *nothing*, and decided it must mean I was over her. I had left her on Sunday. On Monday, I had left the country. Late Tuesday night, I arrived in France, where I would be staying for the next seven months (if not longer). On Wednesday, I moved into my apartment. On Thursday, I went to a big party in the town— everyone was excited to the see the *American*, and I must have been passably interesting (interesting *enough*) for one of them to invite me to a *soirée* the next night. On Friday, I went to the next town over, in order to get internet for my apartment. Coming back on the train, I decided that I might—really— be over her: when I thought of her, I didn't miss her at *all*. There were three possibilities for explaining how I felt: *shock*, because I had too much to deal with in the present, and the pain would come; I was actually so *extraordinary* that I could break down in tears one day, and then be rather okay with it a few days later; or, I had never *really* loved her that much, but had just become good at *acting*, or at living fully in the *moment*. I was not so blind as to ignore the first (and truest) possibility, but I was not so open and aware as to keep myself from gravitating towards the latter two explanations. Later that night—at the gathering—I was not only uninteresting, but uncommunicative and sullen. I didn't want to be there, and no one would have really wanted to keep me there, either…

Then, there was that moment—three weeks after (three weeks after coming to *France*, three weeks after breaking *up*)—when I finally sent her an email, of my own accord. (She had already sent me one, but—as I told her—*I can't write back and forth…at least not right now…*) It was a long, four-page email that I sent, filled with all the things that I was *bursting* to tell her—an email (to be honest) not devoid either of *grief* over the end, or of a lingering, persisting *hope*, that there still might be an *us* to be grieving over. That night, I had a dream, one which showed me—without *sadness*—leaving her behind. That had to mean I was *over* her, I decided. The next day, I wrote another excessively long email, though this one telling her that it was over—that it had to be over—and we couldn't hold out *hope*, any longer. I cut my hair, that day—the long hair I had kept, mostly because *she* loved it. It was like a *purging* and a new *start* (I thought to myself): starting a new life—*here*—and leaving most everything from my old life *behind*. The next night, I lay in my bed for hours and rehashed—in every minute detail I could remember—all the *memories* I had of her. I cried, and thought that my tears were *joyous*—for what I *had* had—instead of *painful* (for what I had no *longer*...)

Then, there was that moment—in November—when I went to a film screening (in English) in the town theater. The screening had been arranged by the school, and so there I was—an *American*, sitting in a *French* movie theater, watching an *American* film—and surrounded by at least a hundred *lycée* students, most of whom would need subtitles in order to understand the story. After the film, I walked around the town, and eventually sat down on a bench—one that was half-way up the mountain, just in front of the cemetery. It was my favorite spot in the town, giving you a beautiful view out over everything. I sat down and started to write a letter to a friend, telling her about the film—how it had *moved* me so much, and had almost made me *cry*—and how I was *crying* at that moment, thinking about the film, and looking out over the town. I was *happy* that day, and it felt to me like I had finally come back to *life*, had finally woken up from that *daze*—always either numb or painful—which I had been in, since I had left her that Sunday afternoon. The next day, the feeling was gone. Nothing similar would come back for the next several weeks, to break that *daze* which had re-descended—even more heavily—upon me...

Then, there was that moment—late in December—when I was *enraged* by something she had written: "*Everyone said that you'd be a wreck without me, that you never could have made it through last year without me...*" I read that, and my first reaction was to *dismiss* it, because I knew that I was so much stronger than "*everyone*" was giving me credit for. I *would've* made it through last year without her—I *had* made it through all but two months of last year, without her. And I was not a wreck—*now*, without *her*—even if I wasn't (admittedly) as *happy* as I could be. Then, the more I thought about those words (I didn't have much else to think about), the more they started to *dig* into me, and to make me *angry*—*really* angry. By the end, I found myself writing page after page of unending *rants*—against the *words*; against the *people* who had said them; against *her*, for believing them. At some point (my rage cresting), I heard the *click* in my head, and I could no longer deny that these words meant too *much* to me, because (obviously) they were too *true*...

A day or two after that—at a Christmas party—I was talking to someone, and he asked if I had a girlfriend. I told him that I *had* one, but not anymore. "*Tu l'aimais?*" (*Did you love her?*) I sighed—looked up—and didn't say anything. "*It's not an easy question,*" he added. (*Ce n'est pas une question facile...*) After a moment, I told him, "*Oui, je pense.*" (*Yes, I think so...*) All I had wanted, for three months, was for someone—*anyone*—to ask me about her, even something as brief as that *tête-à-tête* was. It's like it wasn't *real*, until that moment—until the thought had gained form and *substance*, in being pronounced to the *world*. Until I actually *spoke* about it—to someone, *anyone*—it all felt like it had been a *dream* (our relationship, or the time since?), from which I would some day *awake*...

After that, I stopped telling myself I was over her. Or—at least—I stopped *believing* myself, when I said those words. I still hadn't moved on, and I still wouldn't, for a long time. I was still combing through memories, still looking at pictures of the past, still visiting her Facebook page far too often, because I just couldn't stop myself. I could no longer deny, however, the broken remains of my feelings, nor the ways that I had tried (unsuccessfully) to build *new* structures on top of them—trying to hide the *old* ones, completely from view. (*I can't remember not liking you...*)

It shouldn't have been surprising, really. I did the same thing *after* the relationship ended, as I had done *before* it even started. I could never get my head around the idea that—all the time I had liked her (those four months, before I *said* anything)—she had liked me, *too*. There had been clues (sometimes, rather clear and *obvious* ones), but I just kept on spinning elaborate—

ingenious—interpretations, about how she didn't like me. They had to be complex and persuasive, after all, if they were going to trick me into thinking that she didn't *like* me, or (and this one was always more believable) that she didn't like me, *anymore*. Neither *before* love, nor *after* love—and, oftentimes, not even in the *middle* of love—can I admit what I am feeling, and see it *clearly*. Maybe that has something to do with *love*, itself. (*Maybe...*) But it undoubtedly has something to do (*much* to do) with *me*—and who *I* am—and just how *pathetic*, *blinded*, and swayed by *fear* I am, in all the stages of *love* and *loss*...

We are our own worst *enemies*, when it comes to trying to see ourselves clearly. As if the tools and insights that we gain in seeking out *honesty*, soon become the unimpeachable means through which we *lie* to ourselves—more and more thoroughly—and then fail to *see* through those self-deceptions. I had forgotten (I *always* forget) that you have to question *everything*, especially what you don't *want* to question—that you have to seek out, especially, what you don't *want* to seek—because *pain* is the only signpost there is, on the path to *honesty*. (But then I was already *blinded* by pain, wasn't I—overwhelmed by the pain of *losing* her—so that I never could have handled that added pain, of starting to see through all my *lies*?) So we stagnate, we freeze, we *congeal*. We forget that we are constantly slipping, backwards and backwards—forever stuck on this endless circle of *ourselves*—no matter how much *trust* we may have in *knowing thyself*, no matter how much we may believe in that *myth* of *self-reflection*...

(*Self-reflection is* selfish...*It's self*-obsessed...*It's self*-indulgent...*It's nothing more than* navel-gazing...*It's independent and* elitist...*It's esoteric and* privileged... *It denies* progress...*It destroys the* past...*It demolishes any sense of* truth...*It's too young, and* idealistic...*It's too resigned, and* cynical...*It's inherently* amoral...*It romanticizes pain and* suffering...*It has a dangerous obsession with* knowledge...*It foolishly seeks out what is* impossible...*It only wants what is bad or* unhealthy *for life*...*It's only for the weak and the* lonely...*It's just a rationalization for* nostalgia...*It's just a justification for* narcissism...*It's too* personal, *too wrapped up in itself*...*It's too abstract, and not personal* enough... *It demands keeping one foot* outside *of experience*...*It leads* away *from life, instead of towards it*...*It's not worth the price that one must* pay *for it*...*It's inherently blind and* dishonest...*It's useless, Useless,* USELESS...*It's nothing like philosophy or* art...*It misuses* religion...*It ignores* faith...*It lacks any stable sort of* foundation... *It reads* into *everything, but only finds what it* wants *to find there*...*It doesn't cling to sufficiently important* subjects...*It overindulges* metaphor...*It's too* "meta" *and self-reflexive*...*It forgets* life, *itself*...*It's* pointless, *ultimately*...)

There are *lost* years, in my life. My life did not *stop*—things did *happen*—but I don't really have many memories of those times. Or, I do have memories of them, but I really have to *try* to seek them out. They do not come to me *easily*—as almost all my other memories do—because (essentially) I do not *want* them to. I have an excellent memory, but even I have to admit this power of *repression,* in myself: both not being *able* to remember something, as if the memory—itself—*repulsed* me; as well as all those the doubts and *distortions* that inevitably creep in, especially about those things that are most *meaningful*, to us. A therapist once asked me for the amount of time between two events, and—for the life of me—I couldn't decide whether it had been two *months*, or two *weeks*. Those two events weren't part of my *lost* years, though—those would come later, when I was trying to get over what (essentially) were *break-ups*. (This is—among other things—a *break-up book*...) Two of my *lost* years came after the end of romantic relationships, and the third came after the end of another sort of relationship—*relationships*—when I suddenly, inexplicably (at the time) lost all my friends...

That was always how I put it—"*losing my friends*." (As if friends were things to pick *up* or put *down*, treasures to be *lost* or *gained*...) In some sense, it was the most *devastating* of the three break-ups, if only because it was the *first*. Between the Summer of 2006 and the Spring of 2007, I was (unspeakably) *lonely*. (*Are we all hopelessly alone?*) Everyone always *says* how much they *hated* high school. But I—actually—*did* hate it (for that year, at least), because I had no one to hate it *with*. I was utterly *alone,* in my hatred—which is the worst way to be, because then you have no one to turn your hatred either *towards* or *against*. (Except *yourself*, and those *closest* to you...) I didn't *want* to be lonely—I desperately *wanted* to have friends—but (for some reason) I couldn't *will* myself out of it. I could barely *survive*, each day. Each day, I used up so much *energy*—trying to keep other people from *seeing* what I was going through—that (by the time I got home), I just couldn't hold it *back*, any longer...

My life continued (on the surface) more or less the same: I did well in school, I was involved in activities, and—towards most of the world—I seemed to have a pleasant (if quiet) demeanor. But we're capable of the most amazing feats of *dissembling*, when we're in the darkest and most *unfeeling* moods. Outside of school and activities, my life was like a *void*—I never spent time with *anyone*, because I had no one to spend time *with*. And I went to the *extremes*, to hide that fact. Friday nights were absolute *hell*, for me, because—as soon as the last bell rang, and everyone began discussing their *plans*—I couldn't help but see (all too clearly) just how *alone* I was. The only thing *worse* than being alone, though, was the *fear* that—one day— other people would *discover,* would *see,* just how *alone* (and *pathetic*) I truly was. And so—instead—I threw myself (excessively) into my few activities. I couldn't make *friends*, so I put my entire will into trying to be the *best*—the *absolute* best—in things like academics and sports. (The one succeeded extremely *well*, but for the worst possible reasons; the other hardly succeeded at *all*, perhaps for the same reasons...)

(*And what brought me—slowly—out of it?* At the time, I would have said *intellectual* stimulation, especially from a pivotal book that I had read. *But now?* Now, I see that it was more like human *connection*, which pulled me out of it—a connection, in particular, with a tall, red-headed *friend*...)

The second *lost* year of my life involved a break-up, in the *normal* sense of the word—my first *love*, and my first *loss*. Everyone knows the story, but that doesn't make it any less important to *tell*. (Or to *hear*...) But I'm only going to focus on the *second* part of the story—the *tragic* half—when love ended, and went away. I was more or less a *wreck*, the last two months we were together. (The *thought* of the end tormented me, and—eventually—brought about that *end*, itself...) And I would be a *wreck*, too, during the nine months that followed. It was probably the *inertia* of life (staying in motion, once we're in motion) that carried me through that time, without too much *pain* evident on the outside. I didn't eat very well. I exercised very little. (I had been in fabulous shape the months before—the months when I was in *love*...) I spent most of my time in my room (the same room, where we had once spent so much time *together*...) I only really saw people in classes and in Quidditch, both of which continued (for me) relatively unchanged, with only a slight drop off in my grades and my participation...

The overarching *structure* of my life had not altered very much, but I—*myself*—had deeply changed. The months before, I had shared my life with *others*, and was *happy*; now, I was constantly *suffering*, and doing so *alone*. The biggest sign of that change were all the *illnesses* I contracted, at that time—pink-eye, fevers, bad colds. My health had been the *best* in my life (the months before), and now it was probably the *worst*. I obsessed over the *details* of our relationship. I fixated on the chronology—the *dates*, and the *hours*—of our break-up. I replayed the memories of us—*over* and *over*—without knowing what I was trying to get out of it. Obviously, I cried the first week or so—after that, I just felt *numb*. I went home for the summer, I worked more or less contentedly at my job, and I continued to try to wrap my head around everything that had *happened*. I couldn't write, for months. And when I finally *could*, it all just revolved (consistently, unapologetically) around this *thing*, which had happened to me. I kept trying to *understand* (like beating my head against a wall of *logic*) what it had *meant*, what had *happened*, why it had *begun*, why it had *ended*. I fell foolishly—*pathetically*—in love, for a day at a time. I sent unadvised emails. I just waited for something—*anything*—to (eventually) come, and to make it all *better*...

(It was only in November—getting ready for a big tournament, and writing a paper on Wordsworth—that I finally began to care about *life*, again: about my *own* life; about the things that *happened* in it; and about the *people* who were in it, as well. *Remembering inside jokes, and horrible weather at tournaments, and dumb decisions on the pitch, and all the Facebook photos that you have from it...*)

The last *lost* year is the most difficult to describe, because calling it a *lost* year is more of an educated *guess*, than something on which I can look back (confidently) in *hindsight*. The reason—quite simply—is that I'm still *in* it; or (if I'm hopeful), *que je viens de la quitter. (That I'm just coming out of it...)* I can't say for sure that this year will have the same *repulsing* character, as the other *lost* years of my life. However, it has (clearly) been adhering to the same *pattern*: beginning with a *break-up*, and then followed by so much *effort*—direct, or indirect (or unconscious)—in trying to find a way to *live,* afterwards. Unlike the other *lost* years, though, this one has been rather *full* (at least on the surface): I took my first step into the *real* world (living on my own, paying my own bills); I worked in a job (teaching English) that I had never done before; I moved to another country; I spoke another language; I made several trips all over Europe. (*But why—honestly—did I come to France?*) Originally, it had been a sort of reaching after the *new*—new *work*, new *places*, new *people*, new *experiences*, new *life*—after graduating college, and finally leaving behind that *old* life of being a *student*. (That *student's* life, the only one—for seventeen years—which I had *known*...)

Only later—having spent a few months in France—did I start to realize what all this desire for *newness* had turned into, regardless of how it had begun. (*To finally admit to myself that there's no going back to college, and I have to let go of the well-known life I had there*...) This was supposed to be a year of *experiences*, and—in its own way—it has been. (*Traveling to seven countries; going skiing for the first time*...) But the biggest *adventure* that I've undertaken this year, was trying to get my head around everything that had *happened*—not only the break-up, but my entire *past*, before that. The most significant *place* that I visited this year was not London, Rome, Geneva, or Prague, but the endless, dark city of *myself*. The most memorable *moment* of the year was not tasting *foie gras*, or being in Paris for *Bastille Day*, or anything related to *teaching*, but simply coming to realize—again and again—just how *distant*, *lonely*, *abstract*, and *scared* I (so often) am. All the truly *new* things that I experienced, this year, only drew my attention—only touched me, and stayed with me—for as long as they *lasted*, and hardly a moment more. My *body* may have been here, but—in a way—my *soul* was elsewhere. (*But where, exactly?*) Still in that parking lot—on a beautiful Autumn day—having so much trouble saying goodbye to you…

In the end (especially if a book comes out of it), I don't know if I'll be able to call this a *lost* year. But in a year which—admittedly—has been spent more in *memories* than in the real, passing *world*, something has been missing. My French, which once flowed—naturally, and confidently—from my lips, has *deserted* me, this past year. So many times, I've found myself stumbling over words, or making the same mistakes that—after only three months in Paris—I had long outgrown. (As if part of me was refusing to admit that I was in *France*—refusing to speak in anything other than my own, *mother* tongue...) I *declined* (pretended not to *see*) so many invitations, throughout the year—even though I was just going to stay at home and write (*Ha!*), or read (*rarely*), or watch (*bull's eye!*) a television show. I had so many opportunities to make *friends*—and to *date*—this year, but I let almost all of them slip through my fingertips. I stopped exercising for long periods of time, but found myself drowning in sports *commentary*, reading six different angles on the same, single game...

(It's my *own* fault, if this year has been less than it could have been—I admit that without hesitation. I probably *needed* to be this way, though—to be *closed-off*, *pathetic*, *lonely*, and *blind*—in order to begin to *deal* with anything. (Or is that sentence just proof that I'm lying to myself, *still*?) As if I *needed* to lose this past year, in order to come back—once again—more *hopeful* and *open,* ready for those deep, memory-making experiences that are the *heart* of life...)

It might seem strange that I spent so much *space*—and so much *time*—writing about the *lost* years of my life. That's more or less the whole point, though: I wrote about everything important— everything *essential*—that happened to me, during those years. Ask me to write about one of the other years of my life—starting from 2001 onward—and I could easily fill a few *dozen* pages. (Ask me to write about one of the *best* years of my life, and you might receive a separate *book*, for each of them…) Ultimately, what I carry over from those *lost* years are not *memories*—like full and embodied *places*, that I can revisit—but *photographs*. A *photograph* of this moment, when I was sick. A *photograph* of that moment, when I could finally smile—genuinely— again. A *photograph* of the first few days, after the break-up. A *photograph* is all that I can handle looking at—and all that I *want* to carry over— from that painful time. That time, which was so painful—*then*—and which still *remains* painful, even now. *(After all, don't photographs record that voie que j'ai pris en voyageant?)* Maybe that's all the more reason, though, to go back to those *lost* years—and to *return* to that pain—*again. (Parce que je marche, je circule, je crée des voies…)* Not in order to *lessen* that pain, but—perhaps—in order to *transform* it. *(La métaphore de se promener…)* To turn that pain into something which might have *value*, beyond the scope of the past *(Does the past lose its value…?)* Something which—if nothing else—can give us a solid *foundation*, upon which to set our feet or our eyes *(You keep me GROUNDED…)* as we continue to walk around and around in *circles…*

The week before the end date that we—that *I*—had set, I sat down one afternoon and started writing a letter (intentionally belated) to her. The letter was a compendium of all my *flaws*: the annoying habits I had *("He was a tremendous show off"; "He hardly ever shared anything about himself ")*; all the difficult traits of my personality *("He was supremely weird, and didn't seem fazed by it"; "Who the fuck knew what he was thinking or feeling, ever?")*; and all the mean or hurtful things that I had done to her (*"Think of the times I didn't contradict your own low assessment of yourself "; "Think of the times I gave you abstractions instead of sympathy and actually thought that would help."*) I was going to give it to her before we said goodbye—with directions not to read it right away—but to wait for the moment (as I wrote on the outside of the envelope) *"When you hate me, or want to."*

It started out explicit and abrupt: *"Forget me. Hate me. Mourn me."* Then, for the next two pages—starting in the first person (*"Read through everything I ever wrote you, and see the hint of horrible thoughts and the supremely selfish being glimpsed therein"),* and then switching to the third *("He was ridiculous")*—it listed all the negative things about myself that I could think of. The more *hurtful*—and *true*—the better:

"Arrogant. Self-absorbed. Distant. Horribly so at times. Often pulling away. Several times on the verge of breaking up with you. He didn't really take into consideration how other people would feel when he pulled away. He could never let anyone into his problems. He could never accept anything from others."

Things like how *"insufferable"* and *"guarded"* I am, and how I *"expected too much of people"*—all those *flaws* of mine, which are evident to anyone who knows me, even a little bit. (*You're a bit of an ass...*) I didn't try to spare myself, at all. In fact, I wanted to be as honest—as *harsh* and as *personal*—as I could possibly be, revealing the cruel, impossible person that (so often) I know *myself* to be.

(That's a pattern, too: I wrote a similar letter—twelve years earlier—in response to a girl who had a crush on me: *"Why would you want to go out with me?"* was the fitting conclusion, *"I'm just a jerk..."*)

"Too much Shakespeare. Too much French. Too many of the same, repetitive jokes. Too much boring conversation." Then, after a somewhat innocuous comment (*"His computer sucked at Skyping"*) and the difficulty that I had hearing her (*"He let you go on and on without being able to hear you"*), the entire tone of the letter changed. I hadn't planned on writing any of what came on the next—the final—page, but it was probably what I had needed to write, the whole time:

"He was leaving the whole time. He was always leaving..."

Yes, I was always leaving. But I was not only leaving our *college* (*forever*). I was not only leaving the *country* (*for seven months, at least*). And I was not only leaving *her*—I was leaving behind the *love* that I had for her, which I couldn't bear to bring with me. I was leaving, *physically*; but I was also leaving, in that I was pulling *away* from our love, and from dealing (potentially) with a long-distance relationship—a difficult intimacy, across space and time—which would have been one of the hardest (and most *impossible*) things that I had ever tried, in my life...

(*Why did he want so badly to leave everything behind, especially you? Why couldn't he continue living without letting go of the things and the people he once was so close to? Why wasn't he strong enough to at least try to hold onto the past and walk with it into the future? Why didn't he want to fight for it at all? Why?*)

That's what this piece was, really. I had thought it was some supremely noble, *selfless* act of love: to give her this document—in order to *hate* me—so as to help her get *over* me. A letter written for that inevitable moment, afterwards, when she would hate me—and would *need* to hate me—in order to move on with her life. Then, later on, I hoped she could look back on the letter as one of the ways—

so many, yet so *futile*—by which I tried to show her how much I had loved her. How I had loved her so much as to rip *myself* apart—and to admit all the *worst* things about me—all in order to try to make her feel *better*...

(*Why did he have to leave? Why did it have to begin? Why did he have to invite you to waterfalling? Why did he have to be what he was: attractive and mysterious, dark eyes and blank face that could have held anything behind them? Why couldn't he have stayed that way?*)

But we can't predict anything, no matter how *prophetic* we may be. After reading the letter (she wrote me later), she was *insulted*. As if listing all these things—these things which made me *me*, and which made her *love* me—would do anything but make her miss me even *more*. Maybe she just read it too early, though—I'm sure she cursed me (and hated me) enough times, later. (As I did, her...)

(*Why did you have to fall in love? Why did love have to end? Why the fuck couldn't he have ever told you any of those things in that last letter, rather than write them, now, when they mean so little?*)

I can't get over you, until you get over me... In between fits of *self-deception* and hiding from everyone and everything—especially *myself*—this past year, there were also these moments of undeniable *clarity*, when I saw just how *true* that sentiment was. *I can't get over you, until you get over me...* Because—even though it had *ended*—it had not really ended, for *me*. I would continue to hold on—until *she* no longer loved me, until *she* had let it fall. Then, she would be the one who ended it—our love—and not *me*. Until then, I couldn't let go—because (in my cowardice) I could only let *go* of something, when there was no longer anything to hold *onto*...

(Why can't you talk to him? Why did he have to fly across the Atlantic? Why the fuck couldn't he have stayed? Why why why why do people come together and then pass each other by?)

The letter was really just to make her *forget* me. To make her *hate* me. To make her *mourn* me. To make her move *on*. Because I loved her—*still*—but I was also too afraid to actually *decide* for that love: either to *end* it, or to try to keep it *alive*. I kept on trying to *kill* it—inventing metaphors about its *life* (as our *child*), in order to bring about it's *death*—because I couldn't let it go. I couldn't let it go, even if *I*— and my own impossible *self*—was the one who had brought about the end of our relationship...

(Why doesn't the love end when the relationship does? Why does the pain last so long? Why don't the tears find something better to fall for? Why did he think this letter would help? It just makes it worse, a thousand times worse...)

§

175

Three years ago (while writing a paper on Nietzsche), I found myself trying to answer that quintessentially philosophical question, of what the *self* is. By the end of the paper, I found myself concluding—not altogether unexpectedly—that (for Nietzsche, for *me*) the self was like "*an empty vessel perpetually filled by ever new content yet which does not exist outside of the particular one with which it is currently filled...*" As if—though we may ultimately be nothing more than our *temperaments*—our temperaments are *many*, and not *one*. As if there is (potentially) no *limit* to the number of *temperaments*—or the number of *selves*—inside us. (As if the *self* were an endless reservoir of *voices*...) We must play at being different than what we *are* (must try to speak in voices other than our *own*), in order to realize that everything— all *temperament*—is just so much *playing*, endlessly filling the *self* with ever new and different *roles*. (But I didn't write that in my paper...) As if we first must *play* at being one wave, and then another (and then *another*), in order to never lose sight of the *self*—the fathomless river of *possibilities*—from which they all *flow*. (I didn't put that in the paper, either...) As if "*Man flows on and every possibility is in him: he was stupid, and has become intelligent; he was wicked and has become good, and the reverse...*" (And—as Tolstoy so wisely put it—"*In this is the greatness of man...*")

§

"When you hate me, or want to." What did that mean, *really*? It meant (and I'm too honest to doubt it) that this letter was supposed to remind her of all the *wicked* parts of me—to diminish whatever sort of idealized *image* she might have still of me—so that, finally, she was *glad* to be rid of me. *(Why did he think this letter would help?)* Ultimately, it didn't matter whether the letter did what it was supposed to do—making her *hate* me—or whether, at the time, it had simply *insulted* her. (*It just makes it worse, a thousand times worse…*) For hadn't that been the *real* goal of the letter: to inspire in her a *negative* reaction—either to the *contents* of the letter, or the *idea* of the letter itself—both of which were so *me*, both of which belonged so indelibly to my (*stupid, ridiculous*) *self*?

But I also can't ignore that other *hope* I had, for this letter. (The *hope*, far in the future…) One day—a year from now, twenty years from now—when she comes back and rereads this letter, what will her reaction be? (That is, if she hasn't—long ago—ripped it in half…) I can't say what her reaction would be, but I can say what I *wanted* it (so badly) to be—*appreciation*, *gratitude*, and maybe even the slightest *spark* from the spent ashes of our *love*. Not enough to make her want that *love* (or me, *myself*) back, but just enough for her to know—belatedly, and beautifully—how much I had once *loved* her (or *tried* to...) To keep a kind thought of me. To keep a memory of what we once *had*—beautiful, if also painful; sweet, if also bitter—*together*...

I wanted (like I always want) to find some sort of *eternity* in love—some way to make it *last*. It might have been deeply *selfish*—at the time—to write that letter. That letter might have been another one of the many ways by which our relationship (and, later, our *love*) was ended—*pathetically*, and out of *fear*—by me, and my own (*impossible*) *self*. (*And yet*....) And yet, I still want, *now* (if she were to ever read this, a letter responding to a letter I once wrote her), I still want her to know—*now*—that I might have been too *scared* to keep alive our love, but that it is only through *disappointment* that we could ever dare to do *better*. That (and this I will believe—perhaps *foolishly*—until my dying day), that it is only from the greatest *attempt*—only after the greatest *failure*—that we could ever go *higher*, and try to do *better*, again. To do *better*—*again*—not only for ourselves, but (perhaps) for *others*, as well...

Writing the last section of the letter (*He was leaving the whole time*...), I was not writing what I *thought*—what I *had* thought, so many times—throughout the months leading up to the end. (*Think of all the times when I said the wrong thing, the absolute worst thing*...) As I wrote, it almost seemed to me—inexplicably, at the time—as if I had started seeing things from *her* point of view. (*He was never a good person to complain to, never had a nice comment or a kind word when that's all you needed to make the day a little better...*) Writing things as I thought *she* might have seen them, throughout all those months. (*He sometimes made you feel inferior and worthless intellectually, always forcing his books onto you and subtly deriding the television shows you watched...*) Writing what *she* might think—later—looking back on our time together. (*Who knew if he even felt anything at all?*) As if I had left behind my *own* point of view, in order to inhabit *hers*. (*Why did he think this letter would help?*) As if—if only for the space of a letter, and some five-hundred, heartsick words—I had tried to put her *self* before *mine*. (*It just makes it worse, a thousand times worse...*) My letter may still have been *selfish* and *scared*, but it also reached out *beyond* my *self*—as far as I ever have, before—in reaching out towards *another* self. (*Going beyond, but never getting there...*)

In the end, there might not be such a thing as *selflessness,* in this life. (*If everything is egotistical...*) But perhaps that doesn't mean we can't—somehow—get beyond our own, *particular* selfishness. (*Then isn't it the same as if nothing were egotistical?*) We always have to be *someone* (we always have to have some *self*), but—perhaps—that *someone* doesn't always have to be *us* (we don't always have to *ourselves*) such as we are, *now*. (*Man flows on...*) I hadn't *planned* that last section of the letter, seemingly written from her point of view. (*He was stupid, and has become intelligent...*) But then we don't *plan* to love things, really. *(He was wicked and has become good...)* Things come to us, and all we can do is to try to *cherish* them—for as long as we have them—before life, our fears, and our solitary, circular *selves* inevitably, once again, get in the way. (*In this is the greatness of man...*)

07.14.09, 09.22.12

(The memories are killing me...)

The summer before I fell in love (the first time), I was being tormented by *memories*. They followed me everywhere I went: memories of my *childhood*, of my years in *middle* school, of my years in *high* school, and (even) of the past year I had spent at *college*. It was my first summer back in my hometown, after having left—what felt like for *good*—on that sunny August morning, and calling somewhere else (for the first time in my life) *home*...

I was now back—once again—in this place where I had lived the first 18 years of my life, but the truth is it didn't *feel* familiar, anymore. Everywhere I went, everything I did, reminded me of some part of my *life*—or something that had *happened*—when I had still called this place *home*. But those memories—which had once felt so *firm*, so *real*, so *comforting*—now began to *repel* me. I would go for walks—to the library, to the Rose Garden, to these places I had always loved and *known*—but when the memories (inevitably) came back, the only feelings they inspired in me were *dread* and *anxiety*, showing me how *distant* I was from everything. I had once *lived* in my memories, because—for a time—there was nowhere else I could *bear* to live. But even before that (and after), there had always been such *reality*—such *sturdiness*, substantiated and corroborated by this real, existing *place*—in my memories. Something *calming* in them, even when they were about the most painful or difficult things...

Now, the same places which—infused with memories—once would've *calmed* me, instead inspired a *sinister* feeling: showing me how all of this *had* been real, but *wasn't*, anymore. Or (what was worse) showing me that all of this *was* still real, but that it wasn't real for *me*, anymore. As if—driving away that August morning, feeling like I was leaving *forever*—I had not only turned my back on my *memories*, but on this *place*, where I had always been able to *find* my memories. (And to find *myself*...) As if I—*myself*—was the one who had changed, irreparably and *unforgivably*. As if I had become a *stranger*, to this place—a *foreigner*, to this very piece of *earth*—where (once upon a time) I had found my *home*. As if my memories were so *distant*, so far beyond my *reach*, because I could never forget that I had left them—and had left this *place*—and now had a *new* home. But (to be honest) it didn't feel like I had gained a *new* home, just that I had lost this one, *here*—had lost all meaning that the word *home* had ever had for me...

Memories—as they have, so many times in my life—were threatening to *drown* me. One night (*My first good run on the cross country team...*), going for a walk along one of the canal trails (*All the times I ran here—alone—once the season was over...*), the memories eating away at me (*The time—in the middle of winter—when two other runners swam across the canal...*), I felt like I was going *crazy*. I couldn't take it (*The times I would come here—after I had quit the team—because it cleared my head...*), either the *memories* would live, or *I* would (*The time I believed—falsely—that my best friend was in love with the girl of my dreams...*), but we *both* couldn't survive. (*The time I walked—for hours—on this same trail, with that same girl, who I had loved, for so long...*) I saw no way out of it...

That night, all of these *memories* (and more) came surging back, and—with their liquid arms— were trying to pull me *under*, where they had once *carried* me (gently) through the past. At some point—for some vital (but *unseen*) reason—a song came into my head. My favorite song in the entire *world*, because of the way it spoke about the *past*, and how that (almost) seemed to sum up the *crux* of my entire life: *What might have been lost/Don't bother me...(And what did those lyrics mean, to me?*) They put into eight words the lesson I had—and *have*—been trying to teach myself, for almost nine years (if not longer...) They're the words we need to *say*, if we are to finally break out of the vicious circle of the *past*, and to start to live—again—in the *present.* (*What might have been lost...*) But they're not *painless* words—or *easy* words—to say. (*Don't bother me...*) When the singer begins to repeat them— over and over and over and *over*—at the end of the song, he doesn't really *believe* them. As if, for the first eleven times he sings them, he were just mouthing the words, trying to shrug off what they really *mean*, and what he's really *feeling*. But, as he repeats them—as the song builds and builds—the words descend into his very soul, and he finally feels the full, *painful* meaning of what they are trying to say. To be honest, though, it's only when the words stop repeating—when they break into a *scream*, one which rips apart the very possibility for *words*—that the singer really understands their meaning. (The only way to mean something, perhaps—to feel it *wordlessly*, after the *silence* has descended down upon you...) I've listened to this song so many times in my life—in so many different versions—even (once) in person. The most truthful part of the song, though, is that—every time it's played live—the singer *wants* the audience to sing those words, with him. (But only the first five—he, in his angelic falsetto, sings the last three, *alone*...) Every time it's played in concert, he *instructs* the audience (beforehand) to sing those words—as if they wouldn't be enough, not without every single *voice* in the room ripping open its *soul*, as well...

That night—walking along the trail—I, too, began singing those words. (*What might have been lost...*) I was *singing*—quietly, softly, but unmistakably—for the first time, in many, *many* years. (*Don't bother me...*) I never sing—partly because I have a terrible singing voice, and partly because I'm too scared to really *try*. (As if opening up my *mouth*, also meant opening up my entire *being...*) For the previous six or seven years of my life, I had always just followed the words of a song (silently) in my head. Even with this song—which had long been my favorite, and the one which would later (so often) bring me to *tears*—I never once had the desire to open my mouth and *sing*, as the singer himself wanted. That night on the trail, though (for whatever *unspeakable* reason), I found myself—once again—*singing*. Singing—quietly, unmistakably, and out of tune—those same, *repeating* words...

What might have been lost... (The *past* was eating away at me...)

What might have been lost... (I couldn't find a way to bring it *back...*)

What might have been lost... (I couldn't find a way to return to that *place...*)

What might have been lost... (I couldn't recover that *calm* I once had...)

What might have been lost... (I couldn't return to that feeling of *home...*)

What might have been lost... (I couldn't let go of the *memories...*)

What might have been lost... (I couldn't let go of the memories, even if I had already *lost* them...)

What might have been lost... (I had already lost them, but it *did* bother me...)

What might have been lost... (It *ripped* into me...)

What might have been lost... (It threatened to destroy me, to *drown* me...)

What might have been lost... (I *can't* let it go, *can't* let it go, *can't* let it go...)

What might have been lost... (Let it *go*, let it *go*, let it *go*...)

And that's where the scream would come. But I didn't scream, that night—I *sang...*

I felt strange, I felt a little *crazy*, but I also felt *calm*, calmer than I had all that summer. *Let it go, let it go, let it go...* That's the refrain I would sing, in the years that followed—after my first love had faded into the past, and after I was still trying to accept that the second one had, as well. But letting go was—*is*— the hardest thing in the world, for me. When I love something, I can't just let it go—not without so much *pain*, so many *thoughts*, and so many *words* (*What might have been lost...*) And not—either—without so much *music (Don't bother me...)* I hadn't fully learned the *lesson* of those lyrics, and—to this day—I still haven't learned it, once and for all. (But a lesson that's worth learning *once*, is worth learning again, and again, and *again*...) That summer—singing those words—I was finally starting to learn it, though. I had to let it— had to let the *past*—*go*. I had to stop *remembering* so much, if I wanted to be able (one day) to remember *again*, without it destroying me. So that's what I did—I simply stopped letting my memories *leap* into my mind, as they had done (incessantly) all that summer. (*Let it go, let it go, let it go*...) It's not that I would *forget* them, entirely, but that I had to let *go* of my memories—at least for a time—in order to start to *heal*, and (soon enough) in order to *love*. (*Your ~~obsession~~ LOVE of Bon Iver*...)

The last time I sang this song (*The Wolves, Act I and II*) was when I heard it live—in person—with my girlfriend. It was the last night we would spend together—before I *left*, before it all *ended*. Imagine it—my favorite *band*, my favorite *song* in the world, and my last night (perhaps *forever*) with this *person*, who I loved. The concert has just finished (and they hadn't played the song), when they decide to come back on stage, for an encore. I know—as soon as the singer starts strumming his guitar—what song it will be. He strums his guitar, and gives us instructions to *sing*, as he always does for the song. I'm shaking my head, though—*frozen*—because I don't *want* them to play it. I'd been relieved when they had left the stage, because—to be honest—I didn't know if I could *handle* hearing that song. The singer has us practice singing the words a couple times, but I don't—*can't*—sing along: my throat is too *tight*, paralyzed by *dread*. The song starts, and they play it— wonderfully, beautifully—with that perfect, angelic falsetto, breaking through each word. But—for the first half of the song—I'm too terrified to enjoy it. There are tears in my eyes (both *then* and *now*), and I feel like I'm on the verge of completely breaking down. Then—just when I don't think I can take anymore—the singer starts singing those eight *words*, those spiritual *convulsions,* those labor *pains*. Without thinking, I reach out and take her (my girlfriend's) *hand*, and I start singing—even though I *know* I can't sing, even though I'm barely holding it *together*. And I *sing*—quietly, but unmistakably—those five, heartbroken words (*What might have been lost...*), as that heavenly voice repeats after me (*Don't bother me...*), over and over again. But when the scream *hits*—when the entire audience lets *go* of everything, and simply yells out into the *void*—I don't scream. Instead, I look over at this person sitting next to me—her face hazily lit by the lights from the stage— and I feel her *hand* in my *own*. (Our *hands*, which always went so well together...[10])

---

10 *Our hands go together well...*(From that personalized deck of cards—*"52 reasons why I love you"*—which she gave to me, before I left. And the one that *surprised* me—making me *break down*—my first morning in France...)

If I ever wrote the story of our *love*, I would start with that moment. Not with the next day, when we tried so hard (and so *vainly*) to hold it together. Not with our last *kiss*—or the last time I touched her *hand*—or anything that had happened the six months before, or the four months before that. I would not even start with that final moment, driving away, when she mouthed *I love you*, and—through the window—I mouthed it back. (*Take care of her please...*) I would start with that moment—sitting in that concert— listening to that song. That moment, when the whole world was *screaming*, but my soul was enveloped by *silence*, staring in the face of this love which was both *there* and *gone*. Which was both *there*—today—and already *gone*—tomorrow...

If I ever wrote the story of our *love*, I would try to make it *beautiful*, but also to make it *honest* (and thus *painful*). I would show how *sweet* and how *bitter* our love was—both *living* and *dying*—and not complete without both. I would show those nine months after (when I was *half-alive*), and those four months before (when I was just getting ready to *live*). I would show those six months themselves— so perfectly imperfect—so overflowing with good and *loving* moments, as well as bad and *fearful* ones. I would show her, and I would try to describe her *hands*. (How her life pours out of them—in everything she does—and how all I ever wanted was

189

to hold them, *gently*...) I would try to show *myself*, and my *hands*. (So strong and fragile—so capable of doing *great* and *loving* things—if only I wasn't too scared to let them reach out, *beyond* themselves...) If I were to write the story of our love, I wouldn't forget all that came of it, and everything that was born—*words, insights,* and *dreams*, *music, books,* and *life*, and maybe (even) more *love*—from this creation, our...

But I will never write the story of our *love*. (*Our story will die with us, as all love stories do...*) Because—in a sense—isn't it already *dead*? (And hasn't it been, for quite some?) Not that I will ever fail to *remember* all that time we spent together. (I will remember it, to my dying *day*...) But don't those memories only *remain*, in some sense, because they're already *forgotten*? (As if the *forgetting* comes first, and the *remembering* only comes after?) The real reason I can't write the story of our *love*, is that it's no longer *my* story—*our* story—to tell. I am one of the only two people who ever *could* write it, because I once lived through it; but I also cannot write it for that same reason, because I *lived* it—because it *was*, in the past—and no longer *is*, in the present. (*There is no such thing as* was—*only* is. *If* was *existed, there would be no grief or sorrow....*) Ultimately, at their core, all of our *words* (and all of our *writings*) are *dishonest*—because they can only ever come *after* the

190

fact, after the experience we are writing about *is,* no longer. (*That for which we find words is something already dead in our hearts...*) Can only come after the experience—no longer—is *ours...*

No, I cannot write the story of our *love* (no matter how much I wish I could!) The most that I can do (and how *little* it is!) is to write the story of *myself,* as the thing that our *love*—that *all* love—has made me. Our *love* itself may be gone, but (in its death) it has gone on to make me—*here* and *now*—what I am, and to give me *life,* again. And also to create, for me—once again—a sense of *calm.* It's different from that *calm* which I once had, in my *memories*—that calm of *home,* which seemingly died (*forever ago*). But the *present*—when we are no longer threatened or held back by the *past*—can also become its own sort of *home*: somewhere to be continually found and *refound,* because we always have this *place*—this *now,* wherever we are—to come back to. (*Bon Iver's* music—like *time* turned into *place*...) I hope, with all my heart, that our *love* has done the same thing— has created that same sort of *calm*—for *her.* I hope that she, too, can now find a way to sing—without *despair,* without *tears,* without either *nostalgia* or *pain*—those words at the beginning of our story (*What might have been lost...*), and at the beginning of *all* love stories (*Don't bother me...*)

L'Histoire et l'amour

In *Lolita*, the theme, the texture, the intrigue, the essence is *love*.

The love that stands out, of course, is that heinous lust—that perverse sort of romantic love—that poor, pedophilic Humbert Humbert has for poor, twelve-year old Dolores Haze (surnommé *Lolita*). But that is only one kind of love, and another moves through the book as surely—but as subtly—as the most sexual and shocking stands forth wantonly on each page.

Lolita is Humbert's *lover*; she is also his *daughter*. He genuinely cares about her, as all good parents do, even if this parental love is often overshadowed, or twisted, or darkened by that other sort of love he has for her.

There are these lucid moments when Humbert—the father—shines forth from Humbert—the lover—and he contemplates (but only contemplates) the kind of life he could and should give her, this daughter whom ironic McFate has entrusted to his protection:

> *that first impression (a very narrow human interval between two tiger heartbeats) carried the clear implication that all widower Humbert had to do, wanted to do, or would do, was to give this wan-looking though sun-colored little orphan*

aux yeux battus *(and even those plumbaceous umbrae under her eyes bore freckles) a sound education, a healthy and happy girlhood, a clean home, nice girl-friends of her age among whom (if the fates deigned to repay me) I might find, perhaps, a pretty little Mägdlein for Herr Doktor Humbert alone. But "in a wink," as the Germans say, the angelic line of conduct was erased, and I overtook my prey (time moves ahead of our fancies!), and she was my Lolita again—in fact, more of my Lolita than ever.*

All the overzealous, overly strict measures that Humbert sets up around Lolita's life—both on the road (almost never letting her out of his sight) and at Beardsley (little non-chaperoned time; few, if any, non-Platonic interactions with pubescent or sexually-viable members of the opposite gender)— could just as easily be the work of a caring, yet sternly overprotective father, as the unflinching rules of a fatally jealous lover. This tyrannical bent in Humbert is thoroughly ambiguous, which is to say, two-sided: he desires her—*intensely*—as his lover, but he also cares about her—*deeply*—as his child.

At the end of the novel, when the moment of revenge is finally upon him, Humbert tries desperately to make his victim understand the reason for his vengeance. "*She was my child, Quilty,*" he says. Not his lover, not his one-day hoped for wife, not his perfect little sex-addled nymphet, with eyes of grey and russet skin, but his *child*. *"You see, I am her father,"* and it is as a father that he seeks revenge, on the one who took his daughter from him and carried her—unprotected and alone—into the wide, cruel world.

Of course, perhaps we should not be trusting anything that poor, concealing, obscuring, memory-weakened, creatively-fevered, testimony-leaving Humbert says. But if Humbert Humbert has not been humanized over the course of the novel; if, after reading some two-hundred fifty pages of his well-placed, ripening words, the reader does not admit some final and important honesty in everything that all-too-human Humbert undertakes and undergoes, then I (unlike Humbert) am left silent, with nothing more to say.

For better or for worse, I believe that Humbert— monster and madman—loved Lolita like a parent loves a child, despite all the unforgiveable things he also did to her. His closing words—apparently written a few days before his death—are those of a father to a daughter, as much as they are of a spurned lover to an unceasing and eternal beloved:

Be true to your Dick. Do not let other fellows touch you. Do not talk to strangers. I hope you will love your baby. I hope it will be a boy. That husband of yours, I hope, will always treat you well, because otherwise my specter shall come at him, like black smoke, like a demented giant, and pull him apart nerve by nerve. And do not pity C. Q. One had to choose between him and H.H., and one wanted H.H. to exist at least a couple of months longer, so as to have him make you live in the minds of later generations. I am thinking of aurochs and angels, the secret of durable pigments, prophetic sonnets, the refuge of art. And this is the only immortality you and I may share, my Lolita.

No matter how ironic and un-authorly the introductory preface by *John Ray, Jr., Ph.D.* may be, I do not think Nabokov, or any thoughtful writer, could ever disagree—could ever fail to desire, with all his or her heart—the eternal hope expressed in its concluding line: *"'Lolita' should make all of us— parents, social workers, educators—apply ourselves with still greater vigilance and vision to the task of bringing up a better generation in a safer world."*

Despite whatever crimes, or violences, or sins the book contains, *Lolita* is ultimately nothing but a book about *love*. About the two sides—opposing and often incompatible—of love: when we love someone for our own desires or needs, and when we love them for *their* own. It is beautiful to be a lover, but it can also be *selfish*—blindly seeking out our own ends—and potentially *harmful* to the one we love. Parental love, too, carries with it just as much *ego* as the most exalted and romantic, and just as much potential for pain and suffering. But it also does everything out of an undying *care* for another, for whom you would gladly give up your life—not hesitating for a second, about spending the rest of your days in prison—if it means bringing about revenge and *justice* on the one who took them from you, who took them away from your loving protection and abandoned them in a darkly-spinning world.

All love has something of the lover and of the parent in it, no matter how intolerable and disturbing that may sound. But if there is one thing that *Lolita* and Humbert Humbert has shown us, it's that there is truth to be found in what makes us cringe, and that love—even the most depraved—can carry something noble and unconditional in it. *(You read the nutrition facts on M&Ms to put us to sleep...)*

07.22.13, 01.11.09

(I open at the close…)

It doesn't take much for me to fall in love with something—I just have to be leaving it behind. My life is like a movement towards the last line of the story or chapter. (In my *life*, as in my *work*…) There are too many instances to count where I only let myself *love*—only realize my feelings and fully *embrace* them—when the *end* starts coming into sight. When I see that it's *water* (as I fly over the Atlantic), and not *land*, underneath my feet…

§

She and I still knew each other more through the veils of *idealization* and *romanticism* than through actual *friendship*. (We had once dated—long ago—before I had entered that *dark* mood in high school…) We were both home on break, having just returned from our first semesters away at college. (My college, which I had first become interested in, because *she* was interested in it, too…) Inevitably, we felt *changed*, after the first months in our new, collegiate lives. (And we *were* changed—though probably not in the ways that we thought…)

As for me, I had recently had one of those grand, unforgettable insights[11] after which everything feels *different*. I felt *empty*, afterwards, but it wasn't the

---

11 *The self is nothing, I am only what I give away…*

sort of *emptiness* that's unpleasant. It was more like a pervasive *gentleness* throughout my entire body, like I was small, light, and airy—almost *nothing*. There was *nothing* in me that was pushing me, pulling me, driving me this way or that. I still did things (ate, talked, read), and I still *wanted* to do them, but there was this calmness and *patience* in everything that I did, and towards everyone I interacted with. I always felt slightly *cold*, as if I had forgotten until that moment that I had *skin*. Now, I had this slightly ticklish *sensation*, constantly on my skin—feeling every gust of *wind*, noticing even the slightest change of *temperature*, between rooms...

I had a lot of free time, on break. I probably worked three or four days a week, and then—the rest of the time—I mostly spent reading. I read *Anna Karenina*, and then—before returning to school—I started reading *King Lear*. Normally, I would have had trouble reading a 900-page book like Tolstoy's—not in the actual act of *reading*, but in the daunting *thought* of beginning such an enormous and time-consuming project. It was easy, though—and *pleasant*—*"to fill the hour"* (as Emerson would say): to read one page, and then the next, and then the next, following the lives of the characters as they unfolded before me. She would also tell me (on this walk, if I remember correctly) how much Levin—the largely-forgotten co-protagonist of the novel—reminded her of me. (*Levin—that awkward, brooding individual, who must find God in order to love his son...*) I could imagine what she meant, but I didn't know how much that comparison (or any of the comparisons which she's made of me, over the years) was really *true*. (One of her better ones: remarking—in a letter—how I reminded her of Elie Wiesel, in the way that we both try "*to hide our smiles...*")

While home on break, I also went to visit—one afternoon—my former high school. I expected to be *nostalgic* and *nervous*, going back into the *past*— but I wasn't, really. I went to see my two favorite teachers, and we had nice conversations—catching up, telling them about my first semester at college. One of them had always inspired me and *believed* in me, and I could never thank her *enough* for that. The other had once been a role model for me, but the sort of role model who you constantly *challenge*, because you want *them*—and *yourself*—to be what you think they *should* be. Only now—six months later—was I starting to see how *unfair* that had been. (To *him*, and to *myself*...) That day, I began to see him less as a reflection of *myself,* and more as a real, living *person*— someone who was interesting to listen to, and who I enjoyed talking with...

Then—a few days before going back to college— she and I went for a walk together. We had arranged to meet at the largest park in the city, which had baseball fields, football fields, a rugby field, a soccer field, a golf course, a driving range, a recycling center, a swimming pool, an ice-skating rink, tennis courts, and several, tree-lined trails—either for running or walking—passing through it. (And also—later—a dog park...) Near the swimming pool and the ice-skating rink, there was a large hill (one that was perfect for sledding), and that was where we met each other, at dusk...

It had snowed a fair amount, recently, and the low temperature called for a heavy coat, warm socks, boots, and gloves. My mother also made me bring a hat. As to be expected, though, I stubbornly refused to wear it. Throughout our walk—traipsing through the snow to an old farmhouse and back—she, too, often suggested that I put the hat on my head. I never did, though. (Some things never change...)

I got there first, as usual. Surprisingly, she was only a few minutes late. As we walked, we talked about what you'd expect us to talk about—mutual friends; the visits we each had made to our former high school; our new lives at college; what we were (or weren't) looking forward to, in the next semester. The moment that sticks out to me from that evening was when we sat down—near the farmhouse—on a pair of steps, leading up to the Summer Kitchen. (Where the farmers would store—and cook—their food, in the Summertime...) My gloves were wet, from touching the snow—hers weren't...

She told me that her grandmother wasn't doing well, and probably wouldn't be around much longer. In a day or two, she was going to see her grandmother—in all likelihood, for the last time—and she had no idea what to say to her. *What do you say, the last time you'll ever see someone you love? What could you possibly say*—now—*that means anything? You tell them you love them, and how much they mean to you*—*but is that enough? Is that just bringing up the looming, impending* Something, *which they*—*understandably*—*might not want to think about?*

I listened, and gently pushed forward (not the *suggestion*, because I admitted that I knew nothing, and couldn't speak for anyone else) but—rather—the *possibility*, of worrying instead about what her grandmother would want to hear. Or—if she didn't know what her grandmother might want to hear—then at least to *imagine* what her grandmother must be feeling, when talking to her granddaughter, for the last time. How the feeling of her dying *grandmother* must drown out whatever she, on the other side—the side of the *living*—would feel, in the same situation…

By the end of our walk, it was nighttime. We were walking through snow—a few inches deep—which crunched loudly, with each step that you took. There were lights scattered around the park, and they created this strange *glow*—the light reflecting off the snow, and mixing with the darkness around it. We had probably walked about three hours, before we came back to that hill (*perfect for sledding...*), and drove off in separate directions. Before leaving, we agreed to start writing letters—physical, tangible *letters*, instead of emails—when we got back to college. (*You write beautiful letters...*) It had been a pleasant night...

A few days later, I went back to college. Eventually, the feeling of *gentleness* I had during break faded away, as all things do. As for my friend (because E— and I did become friends, rather than something more), she never got the chance to say anything—at all—to her grandmother. (*C'est la vie...*)

Later—that year—my grandfather died. I don't remember what my last words to him were. I do remember, though, feeling slightly *cold*, that night—even though it was August. I remember how it seemed to me (that night, trying not to look at the corpse) so much less my *own* pain that I was feeling, than the pain (*helplessly angry*) of my grandmother, my mother, my uncles and aunts—and, even, the pain (*Blindness and Death, Blindness and Death*) that my grandfather *himself* must have felt, before the end. Or, at least, that's how it seemed, to me—perhaps because feeling anything else would have been too difficult. (*C'est la vie...*)

11.11.11, 05.29.13

When my first girlfriend broke up with me, she stressed—repeatedly—that she didn't have time to date *anyone*. She was really busy, committed to so many things, that she couldn't afford to spend time *dating*—dating *anyone*—at all. But that *anyone*—so cold, so impersonal—and that harsh, detached *look* in her eyes (so different from the *joyful* one, when she had said *I love you*) showed me the *real* reason it had ended: she had ceased to feel that way—about *me*—anymore...

If it had really been about *time*, she would have said—"*I don't have time for* you, *and it hurts me so much, but...*" But her language revealed what her *true* emotions were, and the real reason why she broke it off: I was no more to her—now—than *anyone* else she could possibly date. I was once again dumped into that massive pool of individuals whom she *could* date—as if I had been nothing more (to her) than a *potential* boyfriend, fleetingly *actualized*. The word *date* also struck me—*tormented* me—when she said it. What we were had always felt like so much more than merely—banally—*dating*. We had never called it *dating,* before that night—that *night*, after which we ceased to be doing anything, to have any sort of relationship, at all...

It wasn't her actions that struck me, or hurt me, or—completely—perplexed me. Her *words* were what plagued me, and what I couldn't get over. (Saying that she wanted to spend *48 hours straight* with me, when we got back from break—and then telling me, once we did, that she wanted some time *apart...*) *Anyone...I can't date* anyone, *right now...*I didn't even care that she had ignored me that last night, and had kissed someone else—that wasn't what was nagging me. (*Deep down, though?*) It was what her words and her actions *signified*—what they *meant*—that I couldn't understand: that our love had ended, that she didn't care about *me*, anymore. She had said I love you (and had really seemed to *mean* it) only nine days before. *Nine days...*I stared at the calendar, and kept on asking myself how love could change so drastically in nine days. How can you love someone one day, and then—nine days later—be *out* of love with them?

Nine months later, I finally understood what those words had *meant*. Or, rather, I had always known—all too deeply—what they had meant for *me*, for my *love*, and for our *relationship*. But I hadn't understood—until then—what those words had meant, for *her*...

§

When my last girlfriend and I broke up, she gave me—as she had promised—a CD full of Taylor Swift songs. We both loved her music, and had sort of bonded over it. I rarely advertise my love of Taylor Swift's music, at least (in part) because I rarely share my love of *anything*. I shared it with her, though, and knowing that she loved *TSwift* was one of those small (yet significant) details that had confirmed to me just how *madly* I was in love with her...

She gave me the CD the last weekend we spent together, and then I took it with me to France. The first couple of weeks, I listened to it far too much. I would just put the CD on repeat—for *hours*—as I read, or wrote, or cried, or just stared blankly out the window, at the beautiful, Fall-colored mountain. (That's really when Taylor Swift is best, after all— right after a *break-up*...) Of course, it wasn't just the *music* that drew me, but also the *person* who had given it to me, and what that CD (coming from her) *meant*—both for *me,* and for *us*...

I loved that CD—as I loved *her*—but I also couldn't help being *angry* about it, too. In total, there were seventeen songs on the CD, but two of them were songs I already *had*. And not only that I *had* them, but that she should have *known* that I already had them—because I had bought them only a couple weeks earlier, based on her own *suggestions*. They were (obviously) two songs that I *loved*, but I also couldn't help feeling angry—excessively, irrationally *angry*— about this *failing*, on her part. Yes, I *knew* that it had been a relatively insignificant conversation (two weeks earlier), when I asked her advice about which songs to get. I *knew* that her long-term memory was not as excessively *retentive* as mine, and that that she had been consumed—at the time—with more *pressing* matters (like our impending break-up!). Yet all I could think about was how *I* still would have remembered something like that. How—if she was going to do something like this—she should have planned it out *better*, like all those dates and special things (more complex and more time-consuming!) that I had planned for *her*, throughout our relationship. I would've loved to have so many *other* songs by Taylor Swift, but instead I was left with this lingering, incessant *regret*—over what I *should've* done—and this anger at *her*, for being the central *cause*, of it all. (*You calm me DOWN!*)

Of course, I couldn't admit to myself why I was upset. It's like the CD was proof of how much I had loved *her*, and how little she seemed to have loved *me*. (Perhaps, also, how little she seemed to love me— *present tense...*) It's like the CD was a sign of how *flawed* she had been—and how flawed our *relationship* had been—when we were together. It would take me a few months to realize that—maybe—it had not been a *flaw*, at all. Or (if it had been one) then maybe it had been born—instead—out of *love*. I hadn't thought about what the CD might have meant for *her*, because I was too blinded by what it meant—so much, *too much*—for *me*...

§

Nine months after my first break-up, I was writing a paper (on Wordsworth) for class. The assignment was to explore the subject of *healing*, focusing on one of Wordsworth's smaller, narrative poems—in my case, "*The Brothers*." The poem (quite simply) is about two brothers—*orphans*—who have no one but each other to love. Many years ago, the older brother had left—in order to become a sailor—and hoping to gain enough money to support, one day, both himself and his brother. The poem itself recounts how the older brother has now come *back* to their village—back to this wonderful, love-infused *place*, the memories of which have *sustained* him, all those years at sea. He runs into the parish priest, who—assuming that this man is a *stranger*—begins telling him the story of *two brothers*: two brothers, who had loved each other—with all their hearts—until one of them left, and the other (in his absence) died, several years later. The priest knows that it's a story with a sad ending, but he tells the story gaily and humanly, because he also knows (in some sense) that the brothers are still *together*, and always will be. The older brother, though, listens (silently) to the story, and then—broken by grief—he returns to the sea, never telling priest who he was, and trying to forget that he had ever known any other life. The whole poem (as I argued in my paper) circles around this question: *Why doesn't the stranger reveal his identity?* Because (as I wrote) if he isn't one of those *two brothers*, then he doesn't have to become part of that tale told by the priest. Because (quite simply), if this isn't *his* story, then he doesn't have to admit that his brother—the only person in the world whom he loved and lived for—has *died*, perhaps because he (*himself*) hadn't been there to save him...

Wordsworth has this uncanny ability to somehow turn the *reader* into the *character* (or—in the case of *The Prelude*—to turn the *reader* into the *writer*), so as to subtly transform *another's* story into your *own*. In other words, I couldn't really write about Wordsworth and *healing*, without going through some sort of healing, *myself*. (*And I washed myself with words...*) Returning to the poem, recently, I discovered that (in my paper) I had actually *over-read* the forgetting—the complete disavowal of the *past*—on the part of the elder brother. (In the poem, the elder brother does admit to the priest who he was—afterwards, in a letter—explaining that he hadn't revealed himself out of "*the weakness of his heart...*") What, then, was that *excessive* (that *personal*) element in my reading, which—hidden in the words of my paper—had turned the simple, honest ending into something grander and more *despairing*: the vision of a man who never—again—thinks of his *past?* (*Yet each man kills the thing he loves...*)

I often find it useful to think of a poem or a piece of fiction as a *dream*. As if—like in dreams—no *time* ever truly passes between two events. (Between the elder's brother's *leaving*, and the younger brother's *dying*...) As if everything that happens—the *departure*, and the *death*—happens *simultaneously*. As if—according to a purely *symbolic* truth—the elder brother *caused* his younger brother's death (the only person in the world who he loved) by *leaving* him. And—if we are truly going to follow the deep *logic* of dreams—doesn't the elder brother *kill* his younger one, precisely through that *love* which had inspired him to leave, in the first place? Doesn't he (*don't we all?*) *kill the thing he loves*, precisely by *loving* it, at all? For as soon as we *love* something— as soon it becomes *meaningful* to us, filling up our *vision*—isn't that also the moment when we realize that it's going to *die*? As soon as we love something, doesn't it suddenly become *real* and *alive*, to us— real, and living, and *mortal*—in a way that it wasn't, before? As soon as we love something—in a sort of impossibly true *logic*—don't we immediately condemn it to *death*, precisely because we have dared to *love* it, at all? Haven't we—ourselves— *killed* it, because we refused to leave it as we found it: so *alone*, so *unloved*, and—also—so *pure*?

In a strange way, it was *her* point of view that I was figuring out—*over-reading*—through the guise of the elder brother. Because wasn't that what her words had meant (*I can't date anyone right now...*), what her actions afterwards had signified (responding—with silence—to the few, pathetic attempts I made to contact her...), pretending like none of it had ever happened, as if (and this was what I most feared) that it had not really been *shared*—had not really been *real*—but was (quite simply) a *dream*?

It was in writing this paper that I finally began to understand what those *words* (*anyone*, *dating*) might have really meant, for her. (*I was not just* anyone, *but she had to act like that, in order to leave me—the younger brother—behind...*) She had needed to reduce me to the impersonality of *anyone*, in order to not think of how much I had meant to her, and how much I *still* meant to her, in a way. (*She tried to pretend that she was a* stranger; *or—since that's impossible—that I was a stranger to* her...) I still meant something to her—and always would—because of what I *had* once meant to her, in the past. (*As if my tears—that new grave in the ground—had nothing particular to do with her, nothing that gripped her heartstrings...*) The only way to break up with someone, though—the only way to get the words out—is to forget the *past* that you had with them, in order to let go of them, in the *present*. (*She couldn't accept the story as* hers—*as* ours—*as* mine...)

Because—in that final moment—if we thought of all that they had meant to us, how could we ever gather the strength to hurt this person, *here*, who we still care about? (*I'm sorry because I know this is weird and uncalled for on many levels...*) If we thought of the past, how could we ever let go of this love, which was once such a powerful and *good* part of our lives? (*I am over you—this I can say, which is good after how many months now, right?*) The person getting dumped has to try to hold themselves together, just to get through it. (*But I am not over the period of happiness of which you were a major part...*) The person who does the dumping, though, has to put on a stoic, impersonal shield, just to get through it, *too*. (*All my memories are real because with you—with love—it is the sharedness of them that makes them what they are...*) That was why she reduced what we had to something so small and insignificant—*dating, anyone*—because she *had* to, just to get through it. (*But if that is dead in you, then how could it possibly still live in me?*) It wasn't painless for *her*, either, even if she was the one seemingly—directly—causing that pain. (*So I ask this of you: did it happen, or was I dreaming?*)

And—in a way—it was like I was elder brother, *too*. Not in that I *forgot* her (or pretended to), but in that I couldn't get out of my own point of *view*, which—if it wasn't *blind* to everything—saw nothing but *death*. I only started to come out of it (finally) when I could begin to take *another's* point of view—not the elder brother's (in which she and I were both *trapped*), but the *priest's*. For (as I wrote in my paper) isn't that how the priest looks upon things— able to see the *joy* as well as the *sorrow*, and the *life* that's present even in *death*? The priest can talk of the younger brother as both *dead* and *alive* because, even though the brother is no longer *here*—even though he was *mortal*, and always bound to *die*—he still remains, in some sense, *living*. (As if life is both a *reality* and— inevitably—a *dream*, from which we will one day *awake...*) The dead live *on*: in our *memories*, in our *hearts*, in this *landscape* where he dwelled, in the *stories* we tell of him—in this story, *here*—which the priest is now telling, so full of *love*, to the *stranger* before him. For that—ultimately—is what love *demands*: to love that which *dies*, to love that which *will* die, to love that to which you have *brought* death—that which you have *killed*—simply in loving it, *at all*. (*Yet each man kills the thing he loves...*) But accepting that impossible *fate*—even coming to *love* it—is what we have to do, if we are ever going to *heal* and to *love*, again. Because—even if we don't want to hear this— love isn't *love*, not unless it first *breaks* and falls apart, and then has to be put back together, *again*. (*Because I will fall apart, tear at the seams, and never be sewn together the same way again...*)

§

I don't know how I suddenly broke out of my own point of view—*blinded, angry*—towards the

CD that my last girlfriend gave me. Of course, like anyone who loves music, I *related* to the songs—as if my soul had been inspired to *speak*, through those borrowed (and preternaturally *honest*) words of the artist. (The *artist*—that deeply *normal* person—who nonetheless has the strange and rare ability to turn *experience* into *art*, and to *express* (for all of us!) whatever fundamentally *human* things, flow through them...) But whether because *she* had given me the CD, or because of the associations that had formed somewhere in my mind between her and Taylor Swift, I also couldn't help but think how she—my (former) *girlfriend*—would have *related* to the songs, as well. (*Track 8—Dear John, I see it all now that you're gone...*) In which case, I would rather have been the one being sung *about*—the one who is being castigated or *missed* (*Track 14—And I can't breathe, without you...*), pined over or *hated* (*Track 16—Why you got to be so mean?*)—in the songs, rather than the one who is *singing*. As if I, myself, was rather that unspeaking center—that difficult *beloved*, or that impossible *ex-boyfriend*—towards which Taylor Swift so often sings, in her songs. (*Track 7—We are never ever getting back together...*)

One day, listening for the umpteenth time to the CD, the thought suddenly came to me—one which I had never considered before—that maybe she *had* known what she was doing, when she included those two, duplicate songs. (*Track 10—I was enchanted to meet you...*) What if she *had* remembered our conversation—what if she *knew* that I had those two songs—but she still decided to put them on the CD, anyway? (*Track 2—You take my hand and drag me head first, fearless...*) Perhaps the goal of the CD hadn't just been to give me songs by Taylor Swift, but to create a special sort of *experience*—to invoke a special sort of *feeling*—when I listened to it. (*Track 6—You and I'll be safe and sound...*) Maybe it was a *feeling* that we had shared before, and she wanted me to remember it. (*Track 15—I was screaming long live, all the magic we made...*) Maybe that feeling was something *she* had known, and wanted to share with me, *now*. (*Track 3—You belong with me...*) Maybe it was a *new* feeling, one that she wanted me to have. (*Track 11—There is nothing I do better than revenge...*) Or maybe the CD was something to *remember* her by. (*Track 1—I go back to December, all the time...*) Maybe it was something to connect us together— for a few more weeks, at least—if not longer. (*Track 12—Can't turn back now, I'm haunted...*) Maybe it was something to keep alive our connection—even after it was ended—within the bounds of *memory*. (*Track 9—And the story of us looks a lot like a tragedy now...*) Or maybe she *knew* that I already had those songs, but she loved them so much—or thought *I* loved them so much—that she included them, anyway. (*Track 5—I was there when you said forever and always...*) Or maybe she just *needed* me to have them, without putting it into words or reasons. (*Track 13—You should've said no, should've gone home, should've thought twice before you let it all go...*) Or maybe the CD was a gift, something which had to be just the way it *was*. (*Track 17—Never thought we'd have a last kiss...*) Maybe it was an *impulse*, or a decision straight from her *soul*, or something from a *dream*, or who knows *what* other force that made her put those two, repeated songs on that beautiful, heartbreaking CD which she gave to me. (*Track 4— You're not sorry...*)

§

Did I know—really—what that CD had *meant* to her, and why she had put those songs on it? (Did I really know what those parting words—of my first girlfriend—had meant, and what she had *felt* in saying them?) I had no way of knowing, in either case—and (I know) I never will. But then maybe what I needed in those moments was not *understanding*, as the ordering of *chronologies*, the determining of *facts*, the uncovering of the reasons or *explanations*—in reality—for what had happened. Early on, I had been *craving* that understanding—*obsessing* over it—as I was just trying to wrap my head around everything that had happened, without breaking down in *agony*.

But the type of understanding that I needed—the type of understanding that *heals*—comes not from the facts we collect about reality, but from what we *imagine* might have been the case, especially for *others*. That's the only way we could ever really know someone, after all—not merely from the sum total of the *facts* of their lives, but from what (we imagine) it actually means to *be* him or her. (The same as for fictional characters...) To imagine what compelled them to *say* the things that they say (*I can't date anyone*), and to *do* the things that they do (*Giving me that beautiful, heartbreaking CD...*) To imagine why things *were* as they were (*What do you want?*), and why things *ended* as they did (*Why did love fail?*)

Ultimately, the questions in life are infinite and *fascinating*, as well as unending and *depressing*. At first, they're the means to our inspiration *onward*—answering questions fills a tremendous and recurring desire that we have to *know*. But, eventually, all knowledge loses its fascination, and what was *new* in the past soon becomes something which—instead—holds us *back*. All answers—over time—solidify and *congeal*, holding us in place when we should always be moving *forward*. (*Can you take a moment and promise me this...*) Soon, our knowledge—no matter how *well* it has served us in the past, no matter how *true* it has been to our lives—becomes the obstacle to our inspiration *further*. (*That you'll stand by me forever...*) No truth is eternally true, no knowledge free from being overcome by a *deeper* and more *livable* knowledge. (*But if God forbid fate should step in...*) Even if something is *true*, it will still—always—be less than the *whole* truth. (*And force us into a goodbye...*) We must learn to treat our knowledge as another step on an ever-ascending *ladder*—taking what's good, leaving behind what's bad—so as to continue upward. (*If you have children someday...*) To know *more*, precisely by knowing what we don't know, and being continually wary of any *final* truths. (*When they point to the pictures...*) Knowledge, not just to understand the *world*, but to know what I know—and to know what I *don't* know—and to always remember the difference between the two. (*Please tell 'em my name...*) We tend to forget that knowledge came from questioning—and must return to questioning—if it is not to turn against *itself*, and against *us*. (*You should've known...*) We flow, and our knowledge must flow with us, as that ever-changing structure through which we most *live*, and are most *ourselves*. (*Don't you think I was too young?*) And me—when I am most fully *myself*? (*You should have known...*) When my knowledge—and my imagination—flows through my *memory*...

(What do you want?)

I'm sorry because I know this is weird and uncalled for on many levels...(You're not sorry...) I am over you—this I can say, which is good after how many months now, right? (We are never ever getting back together...) But I am not over the period of happiness of which you were a major part...(You take my hand and drag me head first, fearless...) I cannot forget the self that I was during that time, so different from who I was before and probably who I am now...(I go back to December, all the time...) All my memories are real because with you— with love—it is the sharedness of them that makes them what they are...(Can't turn back now, I'm haunted...) But if that is dead in you, then how could it possibly still live in me? (Never thought we'd have a last kiss...) So I ask this of you...(You should have known...) Did it happen? (Don't you think I was too young?) Or was I dreaming? (You should have known...)

(What do you want?)

I'm sorry because I know...*(You should have known...)*

I'm sorry because I...*(Don't you think I was too young to be messed with?)*

I'm sorry because...*(Don't you think nineteen's too young to be played by your dark, twisted games?)*

I'm sorry...*(You're not sorry...)*

(*Whaddya say?*)

"I'm sorry."
"*You're not sorry.*"
"I'm sorry."
"*You're not.*"

"I'm sorry."
"*You're not* sorry."
"I'm..."
"*You're...*"

(*The rest is...*)

And yet, in the end, all this *imagining*—all the imagining, in the *world*—cannot truly get us *beyond* ourselves. Cannot get us beyond our own circumscribed *minds*, beyond the physical boundary of our *skin*, beyond those walls that we build up in our *emotions*, beyond our perpetually closed-off and limited *selves*. (Or beyond our *memory*...) Ultimately, our words—and our art—are only so many signs of *ourselves*, reflecting back to us what we always (*eternally*) are. Like you'd say that a *child* resembles its *parents*, and not the other way around. (*And yet...*) And yet, would we ever say that having a child isn't *worthwhile*, just because it does not get us—truly—*beyond* ourselves? (And would we ever say that about *art*, either?) Giving *birth* to a child, *caring* for it, loving it more than you love *yourself*, and knowing (the whole time) that it is going to *die*—isn't that the most selfless experience *imaginable*, the one through which (if anyone ever could) we most get *beyond* ourselves, if only in opening ourselves up—*fearlessly*—to *love*, to another *person*, to *Life*, itself *(again)*?

(What do you…)

"Can you take a moment…"
(So I ask this of you…)
"And promise me this…"
(I ask this, of you…)
"If you have children…"
(Did it happen?)
"If you have children, someday…"
(Or was I dreaming?)
"Please tell 'em…"
(Did it happen?)
"My name…"
(Or was I dreaming?)
"Please tell 'em…"
(Did it happen?)
"My name…"
(Or was I…)

10.13.12, Morez, FR

I want to take your head in my hands, look you in the eye, and tell you over and over again: you deserve to be loved. Yes, there were all these people last year who I knew liked me, and they floated around me, but I didn't reach out and grab any of them until I found you. You were the one I loved, not anyone else. And I can't explain it, except to say that I felt like I knew you, and I loved what I knew, and therefore I loved you. I can only imagine what you're going through, mostly because I've already been through it two years ago in my own way. You finally let yourself love, and then—poof—it goes away. And you have NO IDEA what to make of it and you can't get your head around it and even all the reasons and ideas and everything don't make any sense, so you just go over it again and again in your mind, and you don't see people, even if they're right next to you, because you just feel alone and left behind all of the time. And all the documents you must be writing, letters to yourself which lash out at everyone and everything, especially at yourself and at the one that you loved—that you love.

Nothing, though, can convince you: not any words, not even my words. The only thing that could ever convince you that it was what it was, that someone did actually love you and it's not just a dream that you cry over constantly because it felt so real but now you've woken up to an unbearable reality—the only way to convince you of that, would be for it to come back into your life, for me to magically appear and hold you and prove that it all existed and did happen and people did—do—love you.

(I think soon is the time for you to read that last letter I gave you, if you haven't already)

But that's not going to happen. M——, tears are coming to my eyes as I try to write this, but I wanted so much to give you love, but I also knew that the best way I could do that, would be also to one day give you the pain of losing love. They go together, and they always will. Why do you think I was and have been such an asshole at times throughout it all, pulling away and making you think I didn't love you? Because I know what it means to love and to lose, and I wanted so much to just love you again and again, every single fucking moment, but I also knew that love cannot be what it is until it, also, ends. How could I justify to myself stealing a few weeks or months or moments of happiness from you, when I would also have to leave you with this terrible, unforgivable, unchangeable pain which comes at the loss of love? That I would build you up, proving to you that I did love you, that people do love you, to the stars and back, but then that I would also have to tear you down, reduce you to absolute rubble, to worse than you've ever felt before in your whole, pain-filled life. Don't I hate myself for it? Don't I try to think about you, and what is best for you, without knowing what the fuck that is, because I've done what is absolutely unforgivable: I've loved you? That is, above all, what is unforgivable: having loved you, having opened you up to this pain, which I cannot stop, and which I cannot control, but only look on helplessly as you suffer and suffer without any end in sight.

I would here drift off into some platitude, which I feel with all my heart and soul, about how life is the suffering of great experiences, great pain and great joy, in order to become stronger and more alive, to become that wonderful individual I have no doubt you will one day become. But that will do nothing, even if it is utterly true. What I can't give you, is precisely any consolation, anything to make it better. Because I was the one who brought on this pain, but you are the only one who can get beyond it, one day. M——, I've always known that part of what I was giving to you—regardless of whatever I was taking from you (too much joy to fathom)—was both the beginning and the end, the full experience of a love which enters your life out of nowhere and consumes you in a way which nothing ever has before, and then, suddenly vanishes, without a reason that really convinces you, and you can't understand it, so it must be you, you're at fault, you're the one who sent them away, you're the one who doesn't deserve to be loved, you're the one everyone leaves. Which isn't true, isn't true, isn't true, isn't true, isn't true, isn't true, isn't true, isn't true (sung in Andrew McMahon's voice).

No matter what visions I might have, no matter what beautiful imaginings enter your head, we can't hold on to something already dead. I was destroyed by only a month away from A——, when we were still together, and it broke me for the next 11 months. I was almost destroyed about a thousand times this summer and fall, and I would have been, if it were not for those rare but just-often-enough visits with you which kept me afloat for a little more time. And didn't I break down—in a way I've never broken down before in front of someone—so many times over those last two weekends? If we tried it, I would just break down even more, and you, you would be even more of a mess than you even are now. Because the worst thing in the world is hope, when the hope is so small and skinny that it kills you so much more than a complete rejection ever could. Do you want me to say I don't love you, that I never did? I won't. I will never say that. Because it's not true. Because I believe that you can take it, that you don't need this complete denial of love in order to survive. Because I know that you will get to the point, too many times to count, where you will almost explode, but you won't. You still don't realize what you're capable of. You really don't. You think about suicide, or at least used to, so much, because you let so much in, more than other people could even imagine. But you handle it, you survive, and the tears and words and breakdowns don't ultimately mean anything, because you survive, you become better, and you figure out a way to open yourself up to the world and to love again and again. Honestly, I wouldn't have loved anyone the way I loved you, I wouldn't have let myself, except that I knew you—you—could handle it. Anyone can handle the highs—and ah, so high were our highs!—but so few people can handle the lows, without needing to forget everything and run away and block it out forever. I know what love means, and I know the only way I can love—wholly, ripping my soul in two if I have to—and I knew that you were the same, and I knew that you would feel as much as I felt—perhaps even more—and that you would survive it. That love would make you better, finally, even if that meant hours and days and weeks and months of pain.

I've always known, without having to question myself at all, that our relationship had an expiration date. Not that we might not one day end up together again, but that it had to end—to truly and utterly end—in order for our love to be what it always was, what it always would be. Our love was what it was—so heartbreakingly beautiful—because it was always ending, always on the verge of ending. It forced us to get everything out and not fuck around, to make every single second together so much more meaningful, to not let the other person turn and leave, without yelling and fighting, or without kissing them goodnight. I was always the Senior, and you were always the Freshman, in that our lives were too asymmetrical, one to another, to stay close together for more than this quickly-fleeting year. What if I were born later, or you were born earlier? What if you moved, or I moved, or we visited...? What if? If? IF? Enough. Our love was grand and blue-gray—for me, it was November and December that I felt I loved you best, that tail-end of Autumn when the air is crisp and you look so beautiful in a shirt and jeans. And we made it back to a cool-crisp day, the first day of Autumn, this year. And the weather alone that day, as we were saying goodbye, would have brought tears to my eyes. It was the type of weather I love, the return of an Autumn which marked how long you had been in my life, and here we were, saying goodbye, letting go what we always had to let go. I loved you M——, forever and a year. It's time to let it go. I can't and won't speak of the future: I don't know what it holds. But if, IF, IF, IF, then it has to be something new, not something which lingered on, only half-alive. Forget me, hate me, and mourn me, please. Life is not a romantic comedy, and when I come home, if I come home, you'll be a grown woman, not in years or in anything arbitrary related to age, but in having gone through love, the full experience of love which includes each and every color, having gone through the greatest thing in life—love—, as well as the worst, and having survived, having become more alive.

If I am a writer, and who knows?, what I aspire to is to create something beautiful. But honestly, the greatest thing I've ever done, hands down, is that child we created together. And it was so beautiful because it was so alive:

thrown into the world, with such highs of joy and lows of pain, and alive enough even to die, as all things do. (For some reason, you love me...) *Thank you, from the bottom of my heart—for I could not have made it without you, without having loved you as much as I did, for Maddy, believe me, believe me, please, even if these are only words, and they can't tell you what I really feel, that I loved you, as much as I could. I loved you, you, you: Madeleine ——, who deserves so much to be loved. Please don't forget that.*

I woke up in what seemed like a new world. Everything was the same as yesterday (the same sunny weather, the same hostel in Amsterdam), but also completely different. I woke up somewhat early and got a shower, being careful not to make too much noise or to wake the other guests in the room. I went down to breakfast and had the daily allotment of two pieces of toast, and then I waited to use the computer to check on my bus (later) back to Paris. I did all this (the same things I had done yesterday), but now it was like a whole new world had opened up before me. When I checked out that morning, the person at the front desk remarked how *young* I looked—and I did look young. (I *felt* young, too...) (*You're 5 years old sometimes...*) Later—before leaving—I was on the computer, and I overheard two young women talking (in English) about going to Berlin the next day. Normally, I keep completely to myself in hostels. I'm not there to make *friends* or to *meet* people—it's a bed and a place to stay, for the night. I say *hello* when I enter a room, but then I only speak again when it comes to *politesse*, like turning off the lights. But—as I was leaving the computer area—I suddenly found myself asking those two young women about going to Berlin (where I had just come from). We got to talking, and I learned that they were also spending a semester studying abroad in France (in Aix-en-Provence). We agreed—on both our ends—that it had been a wonderful experience. I wished them the best for their trip to Berlin, and they did the same for my trip home that night. I was smiling, when I talked to them. I was smiling, when I went outside on a beautiful Spring day, in a beautiful European city. I was smiling—without *meaning* to—and if that's not a sign that everything in the world has completely changed, then I don't know what is...

§

I woke up, and thought back to that experience—that *epiphany*—which I had had the night before. (I probably didn't have a *definite* name for it, yet...) I don't remember what I *felt*, recollecting that experience. I don't even remembering feeling much of *anything*, for the first few hours—even though I'm sure I did. (And probably *visceral*, *earth-shattering* feelings, at that...) I don't even think I ate breakfast, but just went to the computer, and continued typing up the remaining pages of that grand project—*catching up to myself*, in writing—which I had begun several days earlier. (*He's young, and foolish, and believes he can get some sort of love/ immortality/truth by putting into concrete, readable form all the notes and insights he has written the past six months...*) I think I just stayed like that—typing, commenting on what I was writing, my legs shaking (even if no music was playing)—for an hour or two, until I was finished. My father had come over, and we were going for a hike that day...

I hadn't realized how much the world had changed, until I left my room—leaving behind all those *pages*, and *writings*, and *ideas*, and *words* that had consumed all my time, the past week or so. It was like everything was *clearer*, and that clarity was something I *felt* just as much as it was something I *saw*. It's strange, but for how much I remember the unreal *vision* I had that day—that *clarity* I could never, ever forget—I remember so little of what I *saw* with it, that day. I remember so little of what I *did*, or *said*, or *thought*, while in that *clarity*...

The next thing I remember was a moment— on our hike—when my father stopped near a particular tree, and began telling me a story. It was a story about how he had once (long ago) found a pocketknife stuck in a tree—in this *tree*—and had taken it as a sign that would determine the course of his life. (*A sign for what?*) A day or two before, he had received a phone call—admitting him to medical school, starting the next week—and he had to decide (quickly) whether or not he wanted to go. He still hadn't made up his mind, and so he had come to this park, both to sort out his *thoughts*, and to decide his *future*. (And, ultimately, to decide *my* future, as well...) It was as he walked through this park that (suddenly, inexplicably) he found a pocketknife, stuck in a tree—*this* pocketknife, which he now held out to me, in his hands—and he realized what he should do. He finished his hike, and went home—both to make a call, and to get ready. (*Ready for what?*) Ready for medical school, in a week. Ready to become a doctor, one day. Ready, ultimately, to give birth to a whole new life (to give birth to *my* life, as well), all of which had been born through that simple, blind—yet oh-so-*alive*—moment, when he found a pocketknife stuck in a tree, and took it as a *sign* to determine the rest of his (and his entire *family's*) life...

I don't remember how I reacted to the story. (Probably not very much, maybe nodding my head...) I do remember, though, how much it had *meant* to him, to share it with me. And I remember, too, how *silly*, how *foolish*, how *blind* I had thought it, at that time. *Blind*, not in having based one of the biggest decisions—of his life—on such a mundane, *meaningless* event. But *blind*, in that he had *needed* such a *sign* at all, in order to express what was—*clearly*—nothing more than his own, deepest *desire*...

Later, on our hike—when I was alone for a few moments—I thought about that story, again. I thought about that story, and about *life*, and *death*, and *everything* and *nothing*, all at once. I looked up at the cliff, in front of me, and at the river, down below, and at all these little black spots—*thousands*—moving in a pocket of water, near the beach. *Tadpoles*, I realized. So *many*: so many that would *die* before they ever grew into frogs; so many that would *live*—for various ages, experiencing such different lives—and then would *die*, too, one day. And the same was true for me. *I am here now, but I will not always be here...I am alive now, but I will not always be...* (I won't even try to describe the *feeling* that came to me as I repeated—*chanted*—those words to myself...) My father came back, and we finished our hike...

When we got home, my mother was there—she probably asked us how the hike was. The only other memory I have of the day is a few hours later—in the afternoon—when I asked her (rather out of the blue) if she wanted to play a game with me. We always used to play games together, when I was younger. (But it was rather *rare*, at that time...) She gave me a strange look, but agreed. (*The clarity would disappear a few days later, after an argument that my mother and I would have...*)

I think we played *Barney Memory* (a game at which—even as a 3-year old—I had always *beaten* her), or maybe it was *Connect Four*. I don't remember who won that day, though. I don't even remember *enjoying* it all that much, to be honest.

By that time, my entire soul was aflame and *shaking*, just as my legs had been both that morning and the night before. The *clarity* of my vision had become something that was *weighing* on me, making me both anxious and *anguished*. I had only asked my mother to play a game with me, because I had needed to do *something*, and I wanted to do something—with *her*—if possible. (I couldn't explain it, at the time—like I just didn't want to waste a single *second* doing something that wasn't *meaningful...*) We played a few more games, and that was it. (*It was forgiveness that I was seeking...*)

That—in total—was the first day of what I later called "*living*," a period of time (lasting no more than a week) when life was this unspeakably *new*, *different*, *sharper*, *clearer* thing. A thing constantly infused with the possibility of *death*, in any and every instant. (*I am here now, but I will not always be...*) All I had to do was think about *death*, and all the force of my *life* surged up—through my limbs, and into my eyes—and it was as if I was *seeing* everything, for the first time. There was now *death*—*constantly*, *everywhere*—in the world. But there was also *life*—*new* life, *more* life—in the world, as well. As if everything felt more *alive*, more *real*, and more *powerful* than I had ever known it to be, before. (Or *since...*)

What was "*living*"? A coming *back* to life, after so many years turned away from it. A *rebirth*—of *myself*, of my *happiness* in existence, and of my very *soul*. It was "*dying*" (the experience from the night before) which would continually fascinate me, afterwards, but "*dying*" was always mixed—inextricably linked— to "*living*," because one couldn't have happened without the other. I didn't analyze "*living*," because there was nothing to *analyze*, really. There was only an *experience* to remember, a *chant* to repeat, a *feeling* to revisit, one deeper and different than any other *feeling* I have ever known, in my life. Above all, it was that clear sort of *vision* which I came back to—again and again—in thinking and talking about "*living*." For two years, the highest goal of my writing was to be able to describe (somehow) what that *clarity* was, through which—for five straight days—I had *seen* the world. (I stopped not because I *succeeded*, but because I gave up trying to express the inexpressible...) Ultimately, that's what "*living*" was (and still *is*) to me: not an experience of the *things* I did, or the *words* I said, or the *sentences* I wrote, or the *people* I saw...It consisted, rather, of that indescribable sort of *vision*, through which everything felt *clearer* and more *alive*—and I, *myself*, felt more *alive*—because *death* was circling around everything (and everyone)...

I had known that *clarity* before, in my life. (*After flipping my star in 1st grade, because I had slapped a girl's hand...After my Nana's death...Sitting in a cafeteria on Bingo Night, when I was 12 years old...*) I would also know that *clarity* later in life (too many times to count), anytime I found myself overcome by a deep feeling of either *love* or *loss*. (And—so often—through *art*, too...) But that *vision*—afterwards—was also something that I could come back to *at will*. For at least the first year after, it's like there was a *switch* that I could flip, and the whole world—so often unnoticed and *dull*—suddenly became so much more vivid and *vibrant*, full of both the shimmering *vitality* of life and the hard *clarity* of death. Later, my accessibility to that *vision* would fade, only coming back after experiences that I had *suffered*, rather than a trick of the voluntary *will*. To be honest, I still have that *vision* ready—at a moment's notice—once I say the magic words. But the *feeling* of that *vision* is so muted, compared to what it once was. I don't even know if I feel anything at *all*—now—when I once felt *Life* and *Death, Everything* and *Nothing*, simultaneously. I sometimes wonder if I've just become *numb* to it—out of custom or habit, or maybe out of a *need* not to feel such *intensity* at any and all moments, of my life. (*I had changed during those five days, but being better in the* present *doesn't do away with the sins of the past...*)

I tried to explain to people what "*dying*" was, so many times. I don't think anyone really understood—or maybe their *silence* simply hid from me whatever sort of *understanding* they did have. I never really tried to explain—out loud, at least— "*living*," and what that *clarity* was like. There's probably a reason for that—we can talk to each other about *death* (even the *mystical* and *impossible* of deaths), because there is, ultimately, *nothing* to talk about: just a blank space onto which we can project anything, and *everything*. But we can never really talk about *life*, especially the vital experience of our own, individual *lives*. That is mine—and *only* mine—no matter how much (and how many times) I try to *write* about it, or to give it away. My *clarity* is mine, and I could never invoke that *clarity* in you— no matter how *talented* a writer I am—by trying to describe it to you. To be honest, all of my writing is nothing more than my attempt to *share* that *clarity*— that feeling of "*living*"—with others. I've learned, though, that if writing is to work as we want it to, then we need to stop trying to show others what we *feel*, and have to trust that the writing which speaks to *us*, is the only type of writing that could ever speak to anyone *else*, either. (*As I once began a story: The past demands sacrifices of the present…*)

How do I end this? (*Flow on…*) "*Living*" was everything I had never let myself want, before it came to me. I had thought that *life* was going to always be something partially closed to me, or me partially closed to it. But then I found *life* again, after so much time spent in the *not-life* of *life*, where we suffer, and can see no way out of our suffering. *Life* has always been this strange lover to me. How I love so many parts of *life*—and so many people— even as I always hesitate to love the *Life* itself, which encompasses them (and *everything*...) I don't know if I love *life*, to be honest. But I think it's okay that I don't know. I think I love *life* like I love my parents—by *faith*. I can never know if that love exists—if it's really *there*—but I can act and *live* as if it were. That's the only way we can live, after all— not through what we *know*, but through the various and impossible *leaps* we take along the way...

(And this is another such leap, but if I can't make it—*now*—then when can I?)

I love you, Life...I love you...And even if I should turn away from you later, or curse you, or hate you— even if, one day, I should leave you behind—please believe me, Life, even if these are only words, and they can never tell you what I really feel, believe me, please, that I will always love you...

07.25.13, Bethlehem

Special thanks to Socrates, Friedrich Nietzsche, Gabriel García Márquez, Jeffrey Eugenides, Ernest Becker, William Shakespeare, Sidney Lumet, William Wordsworth, Bon Iver, Vladimir Nabokov, Taylor Swift, my teachers, my friends, and my family...